J.M. O'Neill was born in Lim [...] city's postmaster, and educat [...] Dungarvan, Co. Waterford. In the early 1950s he worked as a bank official in Ireland, England, Nigeria and Ghana (the Gold Coast). After working in the building trade in London and the Home Counties for over ten years, in 1967 he became tenant landlord of the Duke of Wellington in the Ball's Pond Road in London. There he established the Sugawn Theatre and the Sugawn Kitchen, a well-known venue for folk music. In 1980 he retired from the licensed trade and settled in Hornsey, where he devoted himself to writing. His plays include *Now You See Him, Now You Don't, Diehards* and *God is Dead on the Ball's Pond Road*. But it is for his novels that he is best known: *Open Cut* (1986), *Duffy is Dead* (1987), *Canon Bang Bang* (1989), *Commissar Connell* (1992), *Bennett & Company* (1998) and *Rellighan, Undertaker* (1999). *Bennett & Company* won the Kerry Ingredients Book of the Year award in 1999. He lived in Kilkee, Co. Clare for several years until his death in May 1999.

DUFFY IS DEAD

J. M. O'NEILL

DUFFY
IS DEAD

BRANDON

A Brandon Paperback

This edition published in 1999 by
Brandon
an imprint of Mount Eagle Publications Ltd.
Dingle, Co. Kerry, Ireland

First published by William Heinemann Ltd, 1987

10 9 8 7 6 5 4 3 2 1

ISBN 0.86322 261 7

This book is published with the assistance of
the Arts Council/An Chomhairle Ealaíonn

Cover design: id communications, Tralee
Printed by The Guernsey Press Ltd., Channel Islands

1

Calnan awoke in the red glow of his room, his whole body in sweat: he could feel it gathering on his face and chest and suddenly breaking into cold runnels against his skin. His scalp was wet, his hands. He sat upright on the bed and swung his feet on to the floor with such unexpected force that he groaned. He looked at his thighs, pulled his shirt across his genitals as if they had offended him.

It was a bare floor without even lino or a rug. There was a chair, a ten-year-old calendar on the wall, a wardrobe, an ancient safe, drawn curtains on the windows. And the electric fire, the red glow: the heat elements were dust covered, unused, burnt out, as far as he could remember, but the bulb underneath its plastic coal and spinning disc flickered and sent out the red warmth that gave him comfort. The room was changeless, day and night curtained off, a red limbo. Spare bulbs, six of them, on the floor, stood guard against sudden strokes of darkness. On the floor too, a dusty telephone.

He shivered. It was damp creeping November and he shivered; the sweat was drying, his scalp was cold. Outside, a herd of traffic rumbled past and the windows vibrated. Then he heard the telephone ringing somewhere in his mind; he felt it had been ringing a long time, gradually creeping into his consciousness, prodding him out of sleep. Like a weight-lifter he forced himself upright, steadied himself a moment or two, went out to the landing and downstairs to the bar.

He was all right when he got going, he could walk a

straight line, stand on one leg if that was a test; maybe even reach his toes, he pondered. Then suddenly he was breathless, tense, pulse racing. He stood in the doorway to the bar, looking to where a single pilot light burned on the cabinet, an unreachable haven of liquor. The phone rang-rang with the awful patience and persistence of a corner shop Asian. His pulse was wild. The juggernauts released at the junction traffic-lights thundered past the bar windows, and on and on from hazard to hazard. By his bed upstairs there was brandy; where the light shone in the bar there was brandy; and he was abandoned, a mountain of stairs behind him, a tundra of damp littered carpet ahead. He moved for the bar – a hard swinging motion – wondering where strength came from in his weariness, and snatched the brandy bottle from its holder and drank: a mouthful, two, three, gulped down and he stood by the counter and awaited peace. In seconds it had come, an explosion of warmth: the pulse, the hammer of death itself, fading until he could shape the semblance of a smile, gaze at his sweaty hands. There were good days and bad days.

Tirelessly the phone summoned him. He drank again, brought the bottle with him and, angry and impatient now, went out across the bar, sensitive feet becoming aware of wet and dry, each discard of floor litter: dog-end, peanut hard as shingle, wrapper, dog-end, dog-end, spittle, and inched his journey to the phone – a coin-box mounted on the flock wall, framed in pencilled numbers of whores and mini-cabs.

Ring-ring, ring-ring. He looked at it and drank again, a nip for the road: if this instant of solace and warmth could last forever. Christ, the phone! The clock over the figured mirror said twenty-five to four and he looked across at his reflection, naked but for a string vest and his great belly pushing out against it so that it was raised and his penis hung sadly: he saw stout firm legs, fat thighs, a belly, a wattle of flesh at his jowls and was shocked at the savage ugliness.

'Yes,' he hoarse-mumbled into the phone.

'Is that the Trade Winds?'

He knew Mackessy's voice at once. 'What do you want?' In the mirror he saw himself a brainless comic figure, the chill hovering about his arse, barefoot in a minefield of glass and rubbish.

'What do you want, Mackessy? What do you want?'

'Your voice sounded odd.'

'What do you want?'

'I don't want anything really, Cal . . .'

'Good.'

'Neelan is with me.'

'That's his affair. Do you know what time it is?'

'Hold on a minute.' He could hear Mackessy opening the door of the booth and calling out to Neelan. 'Neelan makes it twenty to four.'

'Christ!' Calnan said, looking at his genitals in the mirror: he dealt with lunacy daily from minute to minute.

'You didn't stand on glass, did you?' Mackessy said with a trace of concern.

'No,' Calnan said. 'Put your mind at rest. Why are we chatting like this at four o'clock in the morning?'

'Twenty to four.'

'At twenty to four?'

'Black news, I'm afraid, Cal. Black as ink. Neelan took it badly. He's sitting here on the kerb, white as a sheet. Hands trembling a bit, he can hardly light a fag.'

Calnan looked at the telephone scribbles and graffiti: '. . . three-speed arsehole for hire, the guv'nor is on the game, can we have a new wall? . . .' The pilot lamp made a pool of light and beyond it a vague crepuscular world. Traffic rumbled past again. Silence.

'Are you still there, Cal?'

'Yes.'

'Duffy is dead.'

From the waste-bin he could hear the rustle of crisp bags where the mice foraged: for months there had been a strange plethora of them, a plague: once in the small hours he had

3

stood still, piercing the darkness until their every spastic move was visible. He had counted thirty-eight. Christ, thirty-eight! He drank from the bottle again.

'Did you hear? Duffy is dead.'

'Yes.'

'Neelan took it bad. Delayed-action shock, I'd call it. Forty-five, same age as Duffy and myself, you see, but of course never exposed to the closeness of death. Death, walking beside us always, I told him. Keep it in mind. I buried the father and two brothers in six months, you know. The first time under fire is a hard passage.'

There was an air of battles royal and combat fatigue about it all.

'Yes,' Mackessy repeated, 'Neelan took it bad.'

'But he's not dead?'

'No. Duffy is dead.'

'You told me,' Calnan whispered dangerously. 'You told me.'

'It's a shock for you, Cal, I know. But I thought I'd give it to you straight from the shoulder. Best in the end.'

'You're looking for a drink, aren't you?' Calnan said.

'Well, I wouldn't say no. And Neelan needs a few shots. We're at the Archway. The Spades have a mini-shop across the road. We could be down to you in ten minutes.'

Calnan's silence was consent. He rang off: death opened groaning sluice-gates of insincerity. Duffy, dead, owed him ten pounds, he remembered. He put the brandy bottle on the cabinet and drank a glass of beer. He was accustomed to the darkness now and could peer into the littered corners of the bar. Five hours ago, he pondered, there had been noise and smoke, confusion, faces, glasses, grins. And there was Duffy between Mackessy and Neelan, the small greedy eyes scanning his universe. He was dead. Ten pounds, Calnan thought, and shrugged. He dried his dank hair with a bar-towel, found a plastic mack to cover himself and went out to stand on the pavement like some lost witless bedlamite.

4

The freshness of the night, of the coming day, assaulted him, brought a moment's strange hunger, sharp as pain, for all the innocence, the virtue, spent along the way. He stood on the corner and looked down to the distant traffic-lights where another pox of gigantic wheels was ready to break loose. Night-time sat kindly on the old street, hiding the scars, leaving a shadow of dignity.

Across the way, a door slammed. It was Cassie, lithe, beautiful, smart as a whip, trotting to her car. The chrome plate on her door said 'Physiotherapist'.

'Emergency, Cal,' she loud-whispered, winked at him as she swung the whiteness of magnificent thighs into the driving seat. 'Highgate before a little handful of rigor mortis dissolves.' She looked at his feet, his belly sheathed in plastic; the giggle was pure music. She rushed off into the night.

Calnan watched her out of sight. The sixty-plus market was the thing, the fiscal thing, she could establish in a wink: disarmed, disarmoured, generous old men – she didn't mind false teeth, wrinkles, wattles of flesh and eyes wrapped in red cobwebs. She had style, Calnan thought.

Down at the Chinese takeaway a squad car throbbed, its kerb door open, and a bulky rozzer with parcels of steaming mush flopped in. They sped away like bandits.

Calnan shivered and went back to the dimness of the bar, turned on the purring glow of the gas fire and felt its warmth on his legs and the dried sweat of his shoulders. Duffy flitted across his mind. Ten pounds. He looked at the counter where Duffy had stood and felt a little sad for everybody. Just a little sad, no more. Drink did that.

He had made the journey to the bar cabinet once more with a growing contentment, was holding the brandy bottle to his lips again when Mackessy rapped with a coin on the window. It came like the sound of a sledge hammer, a landslide into the pool of Calnan's mind with waves of sound rushing at the shorelines of his skull. He blubbered with shock, the brandy splashed from chin to plastic mack to pale bald insteps. He ran, half dived, to the door, pulled it open.

'What are you trying to do, break the effing window, Mackessy?'

Mackessy stared at him.

Neelan's tricky face quivered, set in a cast of understanding: 'A shock, Cal. A blow to all of us. Duffy is gone.'

Calnan looked at him for pallor and trembling hands.

'You don't look too bad,' he said. 'Mackessy said you were laid out on the kerb.'

'I'm holding myself together, Cal. I'd be better off if I could cry.'

'Don't try anything like that,' Calnan warned him. 'Do you think you might make it to the bar? Come on, shift yourself!'

Neelan, sorrow-laden, entered. Mackessy whispered, 'Sorry, Cal. I was just going to give the lightest rap when I got a kind of a tremor. A bit out of control, I suppose.' He slid past.

Calnan gazed with a great crucified weariness at the sky. He bolted the door and looked across at them already ensconced at the fire, men of substance in their picture frame, their Dutch interior gently brushed about them, unassailable.

There was a canine quality about Neelan and Mackessy, dogs of indeterminate breed but instantly recognisable: something of the gun dog in Mackessy, of fair size and working weight, a willingness to come to heel but always the shadow of some dobermann dalliance in the past: he hid behind the placidity of a gun dog's face. Neelan was an undersized, miscegenated chow, the runt of the litter with the important bark of a small dog, sharp teeth when he snarled, leery, unresponsive to kindness. In some human athletic arena they might have been a formidable doubles force with the cageyness and rapport of champions. Blackguardism too. Mean city streets left marks on man and beast.

'Two large brandies,' Mackessy said with hopelessness, as if

6

he had lost confidence even in the power of drink. 'And one for yourself. And mind your feet. You could slit an artery there as quick as dammit. Make them double-doubles. Four shots in each glass. We all need a stiffener.'

Calnan brought the drinks, wary, without enthusiasm, and placed them. 'Before you sit, now,' Neelan said, 'repeat the dose. Double-doubles again.'

'Double-doubles?' Calnan said.

'Yes. And mind your feet.'

Calnan studied him; it wouldn't worry Neelan if he plied hither and thither by clapped-out wheelchair. 'Double-doubles twice. That's eight nips to a glass. Twenty-four nips. There's twenty-seven nips in a bottle!'

'The occasion calls for it, wouldn't you say?' Mackessy asked.

Calnan brought the drinks and waited.

Mackessy seemed to be down some long road of memory and then suddenly back, apologetic. 'I was miles away. Put me on the slate for a few bob, say twenty flags, Cal.' There was a kind of sad resignation, a lazy Sotheby movement of wrist and little finger. Calnan pondered it. 'Take the drinks out of twenty and give me the change,' Mackessy simplified it.

And to ease complication or drudgery, Neelan said considerately: 'Mine out of it too, you see.'

Calnan waited but they gazed with infinite sadness at the gas fire. Twenty-four brandies.

'It came at a bad time,' Mackessy exhaled.

'Eh?'

'Duffy. He popped off at an awkward moment. He didn't owe you any money, I hope. You can't chase the dead, they say. Respect, I suppose. There wasn't a shred of badness in the man. But forgetful. He owed us a few bob, God rest his soul. Publicans, of course, are bound to get caught from time to time. Part of the game.'

Calnan went to the till and brought back the change, the

remnants of this insubstantial twenty, and Mackessy nodded his appreciation.

'This is Friday morning. I'll want it next Friday,' Calnan told him. 'Don't have any intention of dying before the week is out.'

'God bless the mark!' Neelan said piously, making a miniaturised sign of the cross.

Mackessy nodded reassurance to Calnan, brothers in fiscal expertise, men of the world. He raised his glass.

'Take life, take death, take a pinch of salt. To the thinking man the whole thing's a bloody joke.'

'Friday,' Calnan said. 'No joke.' He watched them drink and nod their heads at the excellence of cheap spiked-up German grape juice.

'Good stuff,' Mackessy said. 'Brandy for the emergency. Cognac my father used to call it.'

Calnan wondered what they'd call it in Cognac; and Neelan sang out: 'To Duffy from his butties. Liffeymen all. His Father's House, the Bed of Heaven to him!'

'Amen,' Mackessy concurred.

Calnan gazed savagely into the darkness.

'You have nothing on under that coat,' Neelan said gravely. 'You'll catch your death. I can see your arse through it.'

'And what you had for your breakfast from this side,' Mackessy said.

Suddenly they were laughing, touching glasses, gaping silent guffaws to each other. There was always a great urge to laugh at misfortune, at funerals and corpse houses, Calnan thought, watching them. Fingers to the Reaper. He took his untouched brandy with him and went upstairs to his bedroom and the red fluorescence from the fireplace. He could hear the laughter downstairs; he drank the brandy. Soon they would be sombre, immersed in death again and as the day wore on their hides and minds would thicken against uncertainty and dread.

He went to the bathroom and gazed unhappily at himself

8

in the mirror: he was fifty-six and he remembered the young face beneath the sagging mask; he tilted the mask one way and another to tighten the skin, cupped a hand to hide the wattle flesh at his chin. He looked old; dank twists of hair, black, grey, dripped from his head.

The bathroom was neglected, on the borderline of revulsion. He shaved and sat in the foxed, freckled bath and showered himself, dried flesh and hair until he was breathless from the exertion. He needed brandy: brandy gave you breath and took it away again. He dressed: wore a suit, a tie, clean shoes, brushed back his hair, went to the bathroom to view himself and smiled a little, lit his first cigarette. Downstairs Neelan was wheezing, sucking in air in a drowning spasm of phlegm and bronchitis and Mackessy harassed him.

'Get it up . . . get it up . . . let it go . . . let it go!'

Calnan on the landing roared like a striking samurai, 'Foul my carpet Neelan and I'll break your legs! You hear?'

Only silence. Words echoing in empty rooms. A small window on the landing looked out on the roof-tops of Hackney: old, old roofs and a thousand drunken chimney pots were black against the rim of dawn creeping into east London. He felt a friendliness for it, the smile of one battered fighter to another. He was almost ready for the day . . .

When he went down to the bar again, he saw their empty glasses and the darkness was greying: morning taprooms were acts of contrition, imperfect, but needing forgiveness. He looked for spittle around Neelan's chair.

'A sudden jolt,' Neelan said. 'I went to the john. The whole floor painted in puke! . . .'

'Psychosomatic,' Mackessy explained. 'The trigger, you see. Not everyone can face it first thing. He's back like a blocked airline. I put a paper down for him. No harm done, everything tidy, folded away. I know my way to the dustbins.' Mackessy was unravelling a few crumpled notes and coin. 'Two pints of bitter, Cal, and a drop of cognac for yourself.'

'I'll buy my own,' Calnan told him. 'You should only

squander someone else's money.' He brought two pints of bitter to the table and a half-pint for himself.

'Sit down, Cal, sit down. Take the weight off.' Mackessy said with a great show of kindliness: a willingness to indulge the blinding arrogance of innkeepers. 'The first crack of dawn is here.'

'Death doesn't seem real until the morning,' Neelan said; he stood up and went to the counter, rested his elbows on it. 'Twelve o'clock, midnight . . . a few minutes ago, you could say . . . I was standing here. This spot.'

Mackessy, in the spirit of it, joined him. 'I was here.'

They left a space between them. 'You stand in for Duffy, Cal.' Neelan was arranging it. 'Here between us. When I tell you what he said you'll know the shadow of death was here last night and crossed him for a moment.'

'I can play my bit from here,' Calnan said.

'I wanted you to get the feel of it.'

'Don't upset yourself.'

Neelan weathered the disappointment; he waited for the traffic to rumble past outside. 'Duffy had a bird, you know. Not a bad piece, I'd say. Thursday lunchtime, regular as clockwork, straight from the pub at closing time to her place in Stoke Newington. A Jewish bit, I think, a magician with the food, he told me. He used to sit down to the finest fodder in Europe. Give him credit, he never let her down. A very dependable man, Duffy: wine wasn't his style but he'd down a few glasses to keep her happy. He was like that.'

'Christ,' Calnan said. 'Did he talk to her as well?'

'She could listen to him all day, spellbound.'

'He was careful who he spoke to,' Mackessy remembered. 'And it wasn't every pub he'd drink in.'

Neelan called order, looked at the clock: almost five. 'Thirteen hours ago at Stoke Newington, they're looking at each other across flowers, wine bottles and steaming food. She used to slip away and come back in a housecoat: silk, all flowers or stripes or peacock's feathers, even spots. She had dozens of them. She liked him to show his affection for her in the time-honoured way and of course he was nature's gentleman. But somehow yesterday he wasn't up to it, he said: a complete off-day, no stir at all. And do you know what she called him? A blank cartridge!'

Calnan's face tilted, twitched: their gibes and hokum gave off little peaks of turbulence. Duffy had had a bird; Duffy was dead: they could rearrange Duffy to the heart's content.

'And poured a glass of wine over his . . .' Mackessy paused: death somehow demanded delicacy, euphemism even in fantasy and fibbery, '. . . over the southern region, if you follow me.' They waited for Calnan's deep rumbling, that might be wind or laughter, to subside, exchanging glances of disenchantment.

'And standing here a few hours ago,' Neelan rapped the counter. 'Standing here, he said, God rest his soul . . . "That's the last time Duffy will strip for her!" . . . And of course it was. The last time! The shadow of death, you see?'

'Strange,' Mackessy said.

'The last time,' Neelan nodded. 'He was a strange man. Eyes like steel. You felt he was looking into your mind.'

'You've buried a few in your time here,' Mackessy said to Calnan and the conversation ebbed away. They came back to the fire and drank slowly from their pint glasses.

Calnan remembered dead faces that reminded him of others and went back along twenty years of gravesides and crematoria. Twenty years. He used to vault across the counter then. He was sad and angry sometimes at his captivity. Through the window the faintest grey tinge in the sky was another day to be served. One morning, he felt, he would lock the door on the outside and vanish.

'Duffy,' he said suddenly. 'Where did he die?'

Duffy: mean shrewd eyes, the trace of a smirk; untouched by the merest blemish of work, a contented foster child of the State for almost all his days; always the three-piece suit, fancy shoes, a tie and shiny hair; and some Jewish bird stuffing him

11

like a Strasbourg goose or loading him like a pistol. A blank cartridge, he thought again. Only the poor worked: the unemployed and the rich had style.

'Outside the Bank on the Holloway Road,' Mackessy said and stared at him. 'Duffy. That's where he dropped.'

'He never liked banks,' Neelan said. 'He had no time for them.'

Or need of them, Calnan thought.

'He stopped . . .' Mackessy aped the whimsicalities of death, '. . . like a man remembering something, his hand held up for silence. And then the plug was pulled. An awful sound.'

'And twenty minutes waiting for an ambulance,' Neelan said.

They swapped it over and back and Calnan hardly listened. He knew the insides of ambulances, the red glass and blankets, the cylinders and tubes and masks, the rib–cage pushed and hammered for a hopeful jerk of breath; and the muffled hee-haw of the siren.

'I wouldn't work in a hospital for a house in Dalkey,' he heard Mackessy orating.

. . . Duffy being sped on his trolley, a little flotilla of staff and starch and silence guiding his carrier to port behind screens and machinery.

'They thought he'd make it,' Neelan said. 'The electricity had him going, they thought.'

. . . The whiplash of current to pull him back from death's door; half a dozen bell wires and plasters sprouting on his chest; the screen, a plain horizontal line like the end of a video game.

'We had a quarter of Haig and we downed it. A gulp apiece. I can't stand hospital lifts,' Mackessy said. 'Steel grids and ropes tight as catgut reaching down to Christ knows where. And when we got out there was a flash of lightning, a thunderclap on top of it, that nearly put us running down Highgate Hill!'

'The spirit leaving the body,' Neelan said.

In the silence Calnan studied him for a while. 'The spirit?'

'A strong personality, you see. It runs in families. When my father went, a light bulb exploded over my head in the jakes and there was a crash at the kitchen window that shook the plates of ham on the table. The sash-cord snapped, someone said. But who snapped it?'

'Who indeed,' said Mackessy.

'A strong personality leaves with a battle-cry,' Neelan rested his case.

'And it runs in families.' Calnan went and poured himself a brandy; Mackessy looked at the vestiges of twenty pounds and Neelan watched him. They bought two more pints. A milk float rattled outside; the rumble from the traffic-lights precisely marked off the wasting morning. Calnan slowly paced around the rectangle of counter, in the growing light seeing the dirt left in unswept corners, stains of spittle and beer on ancient counter panels, fag-ends ground into the threadbare carpet. He thought of the cellar below him, always greasy with slops and spillage, creeping glinting mould and cobweb winning the battle, immemorial detritus of long-gone landlords. He drank again, pondered, brought unsolicited brandies to the pair by the fire: he was careful – when his eyes left them, they remained in the mind's eye.

'A gentleman,' Mackessy said with prayerful nod.

'Nature's own,' Neelan agreed. They raised glasses and drank to the 'guv'nor'.

Calnan paced on: winning plaudits for kindness or humanity were symptoms of disease, softening bone, wasting tissue. Great publicans were cast-iron vegetables.

The doorbell rang: three short stabs. It was Brennan, the cleaner. Brennan's time was half-past seven so it must be ten to eight. The clock, ten minutes fast, said eight precisely. The cleaner, Calnan thought, and looked at the neglect all round him, above him, below him. Neglect was like a great tumescent load on his mind.

'I think that's Brennan,' Neelan said. 'I saw his shape in the window.'

'A great man,' Mackessy said, hoping to please: it was a long day yet, a long week. 'Punctual to a fault. Ten minutes to eight. Ten minutes early. A cleaner in a million, a perfectionist. He's been with you a few years. Birds of a feather, Cal. And of course his honesty is in his face. An open book.'

'He was due at half-past seven,' Calnan said. 'And the only stock he doesn't pinch here is toilet rolls.'

He held open the door and Brennan entered with puffed cheeks, blowing out air as if he had made a hazardous journey to reach them; he liked too, to mask late arrival with news of distant events, calamitous of course and diversionary, but bestowing on himself the role of world-weary gleaner and correspondent.

'That was bad in Turkey last night,' he said.

'Was it?' Calnan said.

'A tremor in the mountains. A whole village levelled.'

'That'll take a bit of cleaning up,' Calnan said.

Brennan, grimacing, nodding, made an instant scan of the guests, the fire, the glasses, Calnan shaved and dressed already. And Calnan sober already! It took a share of brandy to bring Calnan from the shakes and depression even to sobriety; he could spend the day chasing drunkenness in vain. There was something in the air, Brennan knew.

'Well, here's to Duffy,' Mackessy said to deepen the mystery.

Neelan nodded. 'I'll drink to that.'

Duffy might have won a marathon or the pools or invented hang-gliding. Brennan scanned the bar again. 'Duffy was in great voice last night,' he probed: '"A wandering minstrel I, a thing of shreds and patches". Gilbert and Sullivan must smile down on him.'

'They're smiling *at* him now. Across the table.'

'Or shaking his hand.'

'Duffy is dead,' Calnan said without sentiment. 'But the

14

buses are still running. And there's a lot of cleaning to be done here. I should take you by the hand more often. I saw corners this morning for the first time in five years.'

'Drink this.' Mackessy came across to Brennan with a smidge of brandy and it was sadly accepted. Sacrifices were made. There was a respectful silence. Brandy and rubbish and ten and twenty pound notes hovered in Calnan's mind.

'The world is a poorer place,' Brennan intoned; and the acolytes at the fire responded in bowed silence.

'We should never complain,' Brennan said: 'There's days when every bone in my body has a pain or an ache. Legs, hips, spine, shoulders. A cripple.' Short-legged from birth he had a variable limp for the mood of each day. 'By the way,' he stopped to tell Calnan, 'she confirmed it yesterday. The missus. August, we think.'

'Well,' Calnan said, 'there's nothing wrong with your tool anyway.'

Brennan limped away; Neelan and Mackessy held ribaldry at a grin; and Calnan looked out through the figured glass of the windows at traffic and people in growth; the Chinese takeaway had closed at last; Cassie's Metro was back from Highgate where she had ministered.

'Duffy. Had he any close relatives?'

'Someone in New Zealand would be the closest, I think,' Mackessy said.

Calnan looked at him and went back to circumambulating his island of counter. 'That's handy,' he said.

2

*T*o every pub its guv'nor and to the guv'nor his sheet-anchor. At half-past ten, with a rattle of keys, Morgan came: brisk, stocky, white teeth always ready to smile; or grin, in warning. Brennan stood by the door for him and announced like a bellman in plague, 'Duffy is dead.'

'Lucky,' Morgan said; he was moving, peeling off his coat, expressionless.

Calnan watched the traffic: its creep and twist was an endless stool with some moist sickly fascination that held him there. Reflected in the window, too, he could see the bar behind him, Morgan, assessing, arranging, planning his day, looking now at the ravaged brandy bottle, lobbing it the length of the counter to his waste-bin. Calnan drew in breath and the long exhalation clouded the window. He rubbed it carefully with his handkerchief: he could see Brennan now, rolling a cigarette, the mop standing in dirty water.

'We shouldn't joke about it,' Brennan said with an air of foreboding. 'Duffy. God rest him this day in the Divine Presence.'

'Your mop's drying out,' Morgan told him.

'Dropped dead!' Brennan said with all the fearful undertones of meeting God with an unwashed soul. 'Outside the Bank at the Archway.'

'Breaking in or running out?'

Morgan called his morning greeting to Calnan, motionless

at the window. It had become an endless gut of traffic now. Calnan, without turning, raised a hand in acknowledgment.

'So the Lord finally caught Duffy's eye,' Morgan said with a trace of amusement. 'That'll keep him busy.'

Brennan glanced fearfully at the ceiling and God. 'Don't gibe at the dead,' he warned.

Morgan said, 'You should change that mop water before it sets. I can smell it.'

For a moment meekness dropped from Brennan and a little poison showed. Morgan's amusement was a burst of gunfire and reflected in the window he could see the twitch of Calnan's face.

Calnan looked at his hands, rubbed them palm to palm. They were almost dry. It took a great deal of brandy to make his hands dry and only a little more or less to dampen them again. There had been a time when there was great pleasure in drinking but he could hardly remember it. Not having pain, was pleasure now; brandy was a friendly household bludgeon.

'There's noise upstairs,' Morgan said and the traffic blotted it out again. 'Who's up there?'

Brennan tried to contain himself with the morning's absurdities. 'Mackessy, Neelan, washing, shaving or something. They spent the night. Duffy, you see, died in Mackessy's arms.'

'Unpleasant,' Morgan said.

Brennan turned away in distaste and smeared a dirty mop along lino tiles at the counter's edge. Calnan watched him: 'You should change that water like you were advised. It's a week old. I can smell it too. And wring the clinkers out of that mop.'

Brennan limped away and flip-flopped his descent to the cellar.

He would sit on an empty keg, Calnan knew, and smoke half a cigarette and gaze sightlessly at his world of neglect and disorder. He watched Morgan stamp on the floor above

Brennan's head to disturb his meditations. 'Send the lift up when you've done playing with yourself, boyo.'

'Another one on the way,' Calnan said tonelessly against the window pane.

Morgan was counting. 'That must be eight or nine.'

'Ten,' Calnan said: he should sack Brennan of course but when he looked at him he saw a junk-shop of cots and push-carts, monstrous disorder and smells, and his wife's face like a brazen death-mask. He left Morgan there, struck in con-templation of Brennan's creeping ménage, and pushed his weight down the bar, opened the door to his living space and stood at the foot of the stairs.

'The whole place is like a bombed-site,' Neelan's peevish voice barely floated down from the bathroom.

'A shithouse,' Mackessy amended. 'Show me a pighouse and I'll show you a pig.'

'That bedroom!' Neelan said. 'The business end of a knocking-shop, red light and all.'

'And the brandy bottle at the ready. Soaked in liquor day and night.'

'At your expense and mine!'

'Not for long more, I'm beginning to think?'

Neelan would be nodding agreement, pointing to the corroded toilet-pan, the dried stains and watermarks of the bath and the handbasin. Calnan listened.

'I hope we haven't picked up anything from that razor.'

'Or the towel.'

'I was watching that. I used a handkerchief.'

'You begin to think of the gear downstairs. The glasses never look too good.'

'Or the bar-towels.'

'Christ, a man could be poxed.'

Calnan listened with the distant icy concentration of an entombed lama; the spiked words brushed past him, had the gentleness of thistledown. He was thinking of twenty pounds.

'He's a mean man, of course,' Neelan said. 'Straight thumbs. A very bad sign.'

''Tis hard to forgive meanness. Not in the nature of our breed. For a decent man we could leave a bathroom like this clean as a whistle for, say, a couple o' ton. Two, three days' work, maybe, without raising a sweat.'

'Two ton!' Neelan made a windy sound. 'For two ton he'd want mosaic and a sunken tub, a high pressure bidet to sluice down the Khyber.'

Calnan listened to them sniggering. He drank from his brandy flask. He could hear the squeak of the lift as Brennan winched up empty crates from the cellar and Morgan saying: 'So the missus is in the club again. Ha-ha! You'll die and go to Hell, you randy flasher!'

Calnan smiled; the brandy was a soft music in his veins. And then Mackessy, in the bathroom, was saying with an air of finality. 'We'll stick it out for this week. For Duffy's sake. But when Duffy is planted we'll hawk our custom up the road. What do you say? There's an English guv'nor in the Grapes now. Clean glasses, smoke extractors, and good evening gentlemen, what will be your pleasure? None of this grunting and bulling.'

'Another thing,' Neelan said. 'It's bad to drink where you can get credit. You're trapped. If you know the clocks are stopped you keep the slate clean.'

'Or if the call comes, dying in debt! A ten or twenty pound load on the coffin! You wouldn't wish it on a Hottentot.' There was a respectful moment of silence. Calnan could visualise the practised outrage on Mackessy's face, the bowed head of Neelan as they plotted. 'Publicans. What are they, anyway?' Mackessy made a spitting sound. 'Drug-pushers, that's the size of it. Make the pub your club. When they're done priming the yobbos for football, it's canisters for the blind, dominoes, darts, piss-ups in Margate and broken homes.'

'Right ... right ... right,' Neelan was interpolating and they rested a moment or two. Suddenly he said, 'I never saw

a woman here and they say he was a ram. You wonder sometimes.'

The silence would be Mackessy's nodding displeasure.
'Himself and that Welsh goat behind the bar, maybe?'

'Or Brennan?' Their hushed laughter was huge intakes of
breath and Neelan's wheeze.

Calnan rattled the doorknob to give the semblance of his
arrival and climbed the stairs, his huge bulk groaning on the
treads.

'Is that you, Cal, old stock?' Mackessy sang out.

Calnan laboured on.

'We're just putting the final touches to the make-up. You
have a fine spacious place here.'

Calnan stood on the landing, looking at them: Mackessy
combing threads of hair, Neelan grimacing at the mirror.

'A fine spacious place,' Mackessy repeated.

'Four empty rooms overhead,' Calnan said. 'Empty as talk
and full of mouse-crap.'

They smiled, nodded, paid homage. ' 'Twould make a fair
hotel,' Neelan assessed it.

'A knocking-shop, I had in mind,' Calnan said, dropping
rough bait like an expert, looking about at them: the walls,
the floor, the furnishings of the bathroom. 'This little place
could do with a lick of paint, I suppose.'

An entrepreneurial nerve twitched for a moment on
Mackessy's lower lip. 'You don't get many bathrooms as big
as this nowadays. A fine bit of space.'

'I'll give it a couple of hours one of the days,' Calnan said
'I have a brush somewhere in the cellar and paint is cheap.'

Neelan juddered in perhaps a mild seizure. 'A couple of
hours, did you say? A couple of weeks, Cal!'

Mackessy nodded, confirmed it. 'A rough job. A professional wouldn't look at it. You could take on more than you
bargained for, Cal. Advice from a friend.' He held a finger
aloft for silence while he pondered. 'I know a navvy, a good
strong lad, no genius with a paint brush, but he's handy

enough. I'll send him down to you. He's at Finsbury Park. Make your own price, you have a good head for figures.'

'I'm not keen on strangers about the place,' Calnan said, ready to set off. 'Stock is valuable these days.' He studied walls and ceiling. 'I'd manage this little box at half-pace in a couple of shifts.'

Mackessy, with slow solicitous concern, finally turned to Neelan who acknowledged the enormity of peril so innocently concealed.

'Give it a miss, Cal,' Neelan advised.

'How much would the navvy charge?'

'Hard to say.'

'Would forty notes cover it?'

Calnan might have said something so outrageously funny that their respiratory systems were seized in jeopardy: Neelan sat on the toilet-pan as if struggling with rock-hard excrement; Mackessy might have been beating on a prison wall.

'Well, Christ!' Calnan said with a faultless show of wounded pride and anger. 'I'm talking to professionals, aren't I? Bloody experts. What would a pair of experts charge?'

They sobered at once, stared at each other, at him. 'No offence, Cal, but we wouldn't touch this class of work. No offence, old stock.' He spread his hands in distress. 'Before we quit the North Wall for Blighty we were top men in our trade. Only the cream of work for Neelan. And when I did the American Embassy in Merrion Square, the hall door and the fanlight, the ambassador himself tipped his hat to me, said I'd make a fortune in the States. Word got round, you know: weekends, people'd come just to stand and look at it.'

'Pilgrimages,' Calnan said.

'All behind us now!' Neelan, adventurer, globe-trotter, said briskly. 'We're a wandering race. That horizon out there is always beckoning.'

'Look, Cal,' Mackessy summed it up. 'The ceiling is sagging like a bellyful of pups. Lath and plaster, a hundred years old. Must come down. Then: plasterboard and skim, emulsion to follow. Walls: strip, make good, line and paper. Woodwork: windows, door, skirting: clean down, fill, sand. Paint: one undercoat, two finish. Resurface bath, toilet pan: four treatments, two gallons hydrochloric . . .'

'Hold it, hold it, hold!' Calnan said.

'Labour: two tradesmen, four days apiece . . . you're talking about four hundred pounds, maybe five.'

'And danger money?' Calnan said.

Mackessy tittered an appreciation of such rapier wit; and Neelan, his back to them, a gesture of defiance perhaps, urinated in a great downpour in the toilet-pan.

'Careful,' Calnan told him. 'That chain, don't tug at it. The whole effin' place might come down.' He went out on the landing. 'Send me down the navvy. I'll give him a ton, maybe.' And then the final cast. 'If you know a good tradesman, it's a two hundred pound touch, no more.'

'Cal!' Mackessy hailed him back, turned almost reprovingly on Neelan. 'Life's short, isn't it? Eh? Duffy with God and a friend in need. A friend's house! What do you say?'

Neelan pondered, acknowledged the way of the world, the quirks of humanity, finally, in peak performance, gestured the throwing of money to the winds where it belonged. 'A friend's house,' he nodded. 'Game ball by me.'

Mackessy held out a hand to Calnan. 'We'll do it, Cal. Ourselves. For you. Two ton. A hundred apiece. Done!'

'I wouldn't want to hold up restoration on listed buildings or the like,' Calnan said.

Neelan's eyes were pale blue alleys. 'There's a half-dozen jobs on the books, Cal, but they'll wait. A turn is a turn. We start in the morning.'

'You start now,' Calnan said. 'Finish at five. Four days, you said. Twenty-five a day at the end of a day. Eighty the top-out.'

'A ton, the top-out,' Neelan corrected, clicked his fingers for exactitude. 'Completion, a ton to come.'

'You owe me twenty,' Calnan told him; he herded them

down the stairs and on to the pavements. 'Material on the nod. Bring me invoices I can read.'

'You could give us ten for a start,' Mackessy blew out smoke at the insignificance of ten.

'Five fives at five o'clock,' Calnan said. 'Now shift.' He closed the door on them.

He'd have a long drink of beer now. The bar counter shone, the cabinet of glasses; the fripperies, the gewgaws sparkled; the neat serried rows of bottles paraded before Morgan's gimlet eyes.

'A glass of bitter, guv'nor?'

He nodded.

There was a faint returning warmth of satisfaction in Calnan's mind. The bitter was cool and soothing. Mackessy and Neelan, shifty as side winds, he thought. A week of touch and go. God rest poor Duffy, the bed of Heaven to him, another twenty on the slate! And up the road to the guv' at the Grapes. What will be your pleasure, gentlemen!

'Christ!' Calnan said aloud.

Morgan gave a stab of laughter. 'Everything in hand, guv'nor?'

'Working at it,' Calnan said.

Morgan's domain, the counter, the piece of floor he trod, his shelves, his mirrors, his pumps, the drip-trays, everything was cared for, the extension of his own discipline and pride: an enclave surrounded by Brennan's creeping dirt. He looked at the corroding carpet, smeared lino, months-old fag-ends and wrappers mouldering under seats: he stood between two worlds and wondered where he belonged. He could dread even the shadow of himself in the glibness and swagger and cunning of Neelan and Mackessy, the slovenliness of Brennan. He looked at the skin of dried dirt, like bitumen, blotting out long strips of carpet by the counter and rubbed his shoe on the hardness of it. Morgan, polishing glasses, nodded.

'Soap, water, scrub-a-dub-dub,' he said.

Brennan. But for the grinding barrier of celibacy, Calnan

23

thought, Brennan might have been a fair parish priest, not overly dishonest or uncaring and with a healthy awareness of Jehovah and his punishments. Had he thought about it once but raging dam-bursting passions had carried him off in his teens? At any rate, he would have learned to console himself that pastors with hops were made and not chosen. His pleading helpless face would have swept parochial polls and, in a world of pulpits, stature could be rigged, and the halt hidden if not healed: he might ponder it sometimes in his mop-bucket; he was the countryman that mean streets had never sharpened. He should sack him, Calnan thought, but always some compassion stirred uncomfortably in his mind.

'Waste of time putting carpets under rubber boots and big loose snouts,' Morgan said. 'When I see them standing in slop and dirt I have an urge to put a boot in someone's crotch.'

Morgan had a little two-up-two-down home of comfort and taste, a proletarian bijou, off the High Road. Calnan had called once and had been handed tea and fruit cake and was at once taken with the strange enchantment of a house, a bastion, a place without shuffling feet or swing-doors or multi-track voices set on collision course. Morgan's bird was London pride: ample, full of sudden kindnesses, menace, protectiveness, and explosions of humour. Cypriots of some origin, next door, had opened a shop: a den of fetid smells, of rancid cheese, tortured mummified sausages gibbeted in the window. Morgan's valley-bred democracy was torn asunder for months on end.

'How are the Greeks?' Calnan asked; all Mediterraneans were 'Greeks' to Calnan.

'Bad enough from the front,' Morgan said; he held up a polished glass and through it Calnan could see a great distorted eye. 'Call it a pong of dung, crap-flies, and Brennan's pisserie fighting for space. But the back! You could meet anything in the back. Tarzan wankin' in the weeds, dobermanns, dustbins, wild cats shagging all night. I saw a couple of goats there once. But they disappeared.'

'They eat goats,' Calnan said.

Morgan nodded. 'Skin, horns, tits and all!'

'They make goat's milk cheese, keep it floating in bowls of whey, it could be. Something you'd clean paint brushes in.'

'Christ,' Morgan said. 'If they farted in bed.'

That amused Calnan; he laughed a little, pointed to the optics.

'A big one?' Morgan asked.

Morgan's bird had long since taken flight to more placid days, and less passionate too, Calnan would guess. He held the brandy in his mouth for a moment or two and swallowed it without effort. Morgan rinsed the glass and began polishing again.

'People had gardens once,' Calnan, hardly audible, said; the noise of traffic thundered when he listened to it and vanished in his thoughts. He knew the nights and dawns of every season in his almost sleepless life: moments of silence, the sound of leaves, birds: London, a rolling meadow, a vault of sky, a hill, a plain. And then wheels and feet rushed across it again.

Brennan came up from the cellar, the same creased effort on his face as if he had tussled with the untidiness of it.

'Everything shipshape down there?' Morgan said tonelessly. He put Brennan's daily drink on the counter. 'Your pint with compliments of guv'nor and staff. You look a bit pale on the cheek-bones.'

'Every year I find it harder to cope with pulling and dragging. That's a damp perishing cellar.'

'You can get piles,' Morgan told him, 'from squatting on metal beer kegs, cancer from smoking. Draw the bolts like a good man and let the public in. It's eleven o'clock.'

Brennan scowled a deep dislike of him. 'Eleven o'clock. Who comes at eleven o'clock? Greasy Gorbals Jock with his tongue out for the slops.'

'Spillage,' Morgan said. 'He comes for the spillage.' His glance took aim at Brennan. 'He could graft in his day, get his finger out, remember that, boyo.'

'Open the doors,' Calnan said.

Morgan took a jug of flat ullage from under the taps and put a splash of fresh beer in it. He put it on the counter. From the doorway Jock locked his gaze on it: a little, famished, rickety man, five feet nothing, grey as whitest silver, a tottering gait as if suddenly he might display an eccentric range of comic gyrations for his audience.

He took the jug of beer and drained it to the dregs with a single lift. That was his trick. He smiled to Morgan, to Calnan.

Calnan said, 'Drink will be the finish of you.'

A little freak gust of wind, before its time, pushed at the door and shreds of paper and a leaf or two lay on the carpet.

Jock trundled away. 'Ach, the summer's gawn, laddie, an' aw the flewers are dee-in'.'

Calnan nodded; he had known him twenty years, more, and thought how decades at beginnings and ends were great sweeping strokes of the brush: a portrait, a caricature. The little dapper man of fifty, mean, awkward, randy; a doddering mossback now, shoe-laces trailing, kidneys weeping. 'The summer's gawn an' aw the flewers are dee-in'.'

Brennan, snout up like a gun dog, said, 'The stink, that man is crawling! Stink, don't you get it?' he said to Morgan.

'Get what?'

'The stink.'

'What stink?'

Brennan faltered at indelicacy. 'Urine,' he said eventually.

'I get it every morning,' Morgan said, 'when you push piss from one corner to another with a dirty mop in the bog.'

Silence settled on them. In an hour there would be a spasm of lunchtime activity and pensioners would soak up heat, sip Guinness like medicine; and so on to the dying fall of midday closing.

Morgan poured brandy for Calnan, Brennan measured his mouthfuls of bitter. Mackessy and Neelan arrived.

'Well, that's that!' Mackessy said, suddenly on stage.

26

'Material in hand, credit like this . . .' He made a gesture of limitlessness. 'Tomorrow morning for the start, Cal.'

'Tomorrow?'

'Tools, overalls, you see. No point in going back to base at this stage. If we saw the beds now? . . .'

Overalls supplied,' Calnan said quietly. 'All you want. Tools, caps, shoes, dust sheets, brushes . . .' Wrapped in clouts of hessian, in dungarees, in newsprint, in Sainsbury bags, he had all the abandoned bric-à-brac of journeymen dossers, unredeemed pledges down the years against a one or a five or a ten. 'I have a hock shop down here for long-distance kiddoes, or experts if you like. Come on!'

A moment of vacuum. Neelan said, 'I can't understand a man leaving his tools, his gear, in the hands of the shylock. To rot.'

'They're usually someone else's,' Calnan said.

'Could we have a couple of pints on the slate, just to get the engines tuned?' Mackessy asked, rubbing his hands. And then to Neelan, 'By the time the material is here, an hour or so, we'll have the ceiling down. Then plaster-board, skim and bob's your uncle. Stage one on the paysheet.' All business, back to Calnan now, 'When the material comes give us a shout, Cal. Don't dirty your hands with it.'

'I won't,' Calnan assured him. 'Come on!'

'A couple of pints and we're there. Two pints, ten minutes. It's hard to get Duffy from hot to cold, from the mind to the box. Standing eyeball to eyeball with death leaves a man drained.'

'Eyeball to eyeball,' Calnan looked at Death's assailants. 'You'll get cash when the ceiling is squared and skimmed. Five o'clock as the clock strikes.'

'God rest his soul,' Brennan whispered distantly in his beer.

They looked at him. Mackessy and Neelan blessed themselves.

'Duffy,' Brennan adumbrated. 'None of us knows the minute or the hour.'

'Five o'clock,' Calnan said. Mackessy and Neelan, morose smouldering bolsheviks, followed him off.

Silence sat on the bar. Outside the wind gusted again and the swing-doors moved. The traffic was endless. Brennan, with a kind of vicious interest, watched every precise movement of Morgan as he tended and embellished his chattels. Calnan returned for a parting glass, exchanged the unspoken with Morgan and, shoulders back, belly forward, strode out into the morning.

Morgan nodded as he went.

Brennan drank a little and went to the toilet. The smell reminded him of Morgan and dislike of him rose up like a sudden vapour about his legs.

3

On the High Road Calnan hailed a black taxi. 'Highgate
Hill,' he said.

The taxi driver, a quirky little man, over-fed, laconic, said,
'Sorry, mate.'

'Why?' Calnan said.

'Not going that way.'

'And I can report that, I suppose?'

'Yeah. Ring the Carriage Office. Tell them I said you was
pissed.'

The taxi pulled away, left him a little dizzy with a hint of
racist blood-lust, and he found a mini-cab parlour. Four West
Indians played rummy, sending out a torrent of noise and
squealing laughter.

'Highgate Hill.'

'Just a minute, me old friend,' one said. Picking, pondering,
discarding, they worked their way down the deck, shuffled it,
sailing close to hysterical merriment and started again. Five
minutes passed.

'Highgate Hill, you said?'

'That's right.'

'What part, man?'

'The hospital.'

'Sorry to keep you waiting, friend. Someone sick, is there?'

'I am,' Calnan said.

'Ah, sorry to hear that, man. You don't look too good, I
thought. Nothing serious?'

'Brain-rot,' Calnan said.

A tall Negro came from an office space behind, charming, greying at the temples, a beard and perhaps the trace of a scar almost hidden; carefully dressed. The card players were oblivious.

He drove Calnan to Highgate Hill. The journey was silent, seemed momentary: remarkable in the absence of cassettes detonating minefields of reggae and drivers, manicured, behind smoky shades and king-size fags.

In the hospital foyer Calnan could only remember that he had glimpsed the football stadium as they skirted Highbury and tracked up through Hornsey Lane and the Archway. No words had passed.

Or money. Calnan knew he hadn't paid him. He thought about it for a few moments. Mini-cab men didn't lose money. Neither did Calnan . . .

The hospital was a vast congeries of scattered, almost whimsical planning, from mourning Victoria to lifetime peers; but the skill of the London brickie had caught all the flashes and facets of Empire zones, torrid and gelid: polygenesis before cloning concrete, the great leveller.

At reception, and with an almost rude tonelessness mandatory on such occasions, he told a cadaverous man: 'I want to make funeral arrangements.'

'West passage. Third left. Management.'

In a corridor, for a moment empty to convergence, he sneaked a mouthful of brandy and felt better. 'PM soon as possible,' they told him. 'Post mortem, that is, you know. Cause of death . . .'

'I know, I know . . .'

'After that, any time.'

'I'll send the undertaker. Keep his clothes. I'll take the rest.'

He signed 'Ronan Mahaffey' for a small brown envelope, a fitting bequest to the universe from Duffy smiling somewhere beyond the hill.

'Relationship?' he was asked.

'Executor.'

There was an undertaker's in Upper Street, managed by the Clincher Casey, for lower end of the market embarkations, and he caught a bus at the Archway. He passed the Bank that would be for ever Duffy's memorial and watched the greasy passage of the Holloway Road to Highbury Corner. Holloway was cheap, Upper Street down-at-heel.

Canonbury Chapels of Rest was closed for lunch but he found the Clincher in the next-door pub, saloon bar, impeccable behind his *Daily Telegraph*, half of bitter, cheese and wheaten bread. The Clincher was a Corkman, of refined enunciation and a whole range of funereal postures and grimaces that endeared him to Calnan. If you took the job on, Calnan thought, you worked at it.

Calnan bought him a pale sherry and said: 'A fellow called Duffy is dead at the Whittington. Died on the road. They took him in.'

'A friend?'

'Christ!' Calnan said.

'A customer?'

He nodded. 'Today is Friday. I want the funeral Monday. I know about DOAs and autopsies, Clincher. All queues can be jumped.' He pushed a twenty into the Clincher's waistcoat pocket. 'I'm buying peace at all costs. Pub deaths, pub debts, the same thing.'

'No next of kin?' the Clincher looked at the clock, at his watch. 'Do you want anything special?'

'A respectable funeral. No more, no less. And your mouth shut. Tight.'

'Has he a plot at Leytonstone? A grave?'

'If he ever had a plot it was a felony.'

The Clincher laughed politely, a moment in disharmony with his profession: he enjoyed Calnan's scowling philanthropy. The Clincher had a pale plump face of some early newsreel of disaster or peeping perhaps from a sepia still of patient ones huddled long ago on Ellis Island.

31

'Cremation then?'

'That's it.'

'The Church allows it now.'

'Do they?' Calnan said; he bought himself a brandy. The lunchtime trade was gathering speed: a subbie or two buying sandwiches and halves of bitter for council clerks living high and wide; in a corner, a studied untidiness of what might be schoolmasters or social toilers; a few gays of course, calm, courteous, precise.

'I should get back,' the Clincher said: it was coming up for two o'clock. 'I often get a call, sometimes more, between two and half-past. Funny, isn't it?'

Canonbury Chapels was ostentatious in its dignity beside a boozer; gold sign-writing on glossy black. The window had a brass cross, tall, untenanted, standing on purple satin and a blue narrow neon tube making a sorrowful patina in the lights and shades; a suspended scroll said, 'Civility, Courtesy, Reverence.'

'Reverence,' Calnan said.

'You'd be surprised,' the Clincher pondered over it, 'at the business that little sign pulls in.'

'Your idea?' Calnan asked.

'Oh yes. A letter of congratulation. The directors were impressed, appreciative.' He smiled. 'I have a great feeling . . . a disposition was the word used . . . for my calling. That was the gist.'

'Reverence,' Calnan said.

'That's it.'

Inside, it was an empty shop: brown lino, brown counter polyurethaned like shellac, brown wood-patterned wallpaper, broad-grained and knotted; a black and gold pedimented doorway to 'Chapels of Rest'. There might be miles of ghostly space beyond it. There was no ceiling light but a standard lamp screwed on the counter: a brass fist holding aloft a torch. It gleamed weakly in the daylight.

'I leave it alight even in daytime. Light has a certain comfort for the bereaved. A symbol of hope.'

'Reverence,' Calnan said.

'Well, that too.'

There was a little glass cubicle at the end of the counter where the unobserved Clincher at his shelf could unwind: a hard-porn glossy, mint sweets, magnifying glass, transistor, earphones, aerosol fly-killer, an evening paper with a cryptic crossword unfinished, were all neatly arranged.

The Clincher entered the details of Duffy's impending disposal in his day-book. 'Name and address of bereaved? That'll be you, Cal?'

'It won't.'

'Ah.'

'You'll think of something, Clincher. Do your sums now, like a good man, and I'll pay you. And don't add anything for reverence and all that crap in the window.'

The Clincher laughed delicately, paused a moment, 'Devine,' he said, 'is a name I like. Bereaved . . . Elmer Devine? Could be an American connection. Relationship? We'll say, cousin.' The business of accountancy was momentary: a figure scribbled on a blotter and immediately effaced. 'Special terms to you, Cal,' he said.

From the fob pocket at his waistband Calnan took a roll of twenties and paid and tipped. The Clincher – charcoal suit, black tie, fragile hands – nodded.

Calnan looked back from the door. The phone had rung and the Clincher's face seemed to melt and ooze into the mouthpiece. Reverence, Calnan thought. He went back to the next-door pub, brought a large brandy to a corner table and opened the envelope of Duffy's effects: a silenced digital watch, a pub diary, a tie-clip, one pound thirty-eight and a half pence in coin. A flyleaf at the opening of the diary, designed as a comprehensive ID of the holder, merely said, 'Name: Duffy, James. Collar: $15\frac{1}{2}$'. Christ! Calnan thought. And a single entry at 1 January. 'I like this sort of weather.' The good intention to catalogue a year's social history had ended there. He wouldn't tell you whether it was rain or shine,

Calnan thought. He flicked through the leaves and found an address in N16. Just an address; and a jumble of numbers that might be a pools forecast.

He drank until closing time, unhurriedly; his palms were dry, no tremor in his splayed fingers when he held them rigid for inspection. The veins were rising a little on his hands and the skin was flaccid: when he pinched it, it sat for a moment like a cockscomb and drooped wearily back to rest. He remembered the old hands of an old man had been like that, age-freckled and loose-skinned; he remembered him, a grey protective yeoman, given to reading aloud, reciting, explaining; always silent laughter; or sending fox terriers suddenly frantic when he took a shotgun from the rafters. Spent cartridges had been beautiful to touch and smell. Calnan remembered a grandam too, a scourge, a harpy, aproned always, and a comb in her scooped-up hair, who had painted God with such merciless flaming weaponry that he had lived in terror of Him. She had an altar in her bedroom, a table really, where she could kneel and pray to painted saviours and saints, giants and pygmies; and a bottle of tonic wine among the graven images had offered him the first warmth and pleasure of alcohol. He tried, with difficulty, to remember her in moments of kindness. She had threatened him once with hell-fire when he had said bitch or bastard. He couldn't remember now. And there had been a day, unforgettable, when she had tied an ailing hen to a cartwheel and ordered her spouse to shoot it. It had 'pip' or some strange-sounding plague symptom. He had refused of course and gone striding off across the fields, talking himself back to temper and peace again. She was not to be outdone. She took the gun, loaded, made careful aim from the kitchen door and fired. The noise was a sudden paralysing thunder but when he had rushed past her the plagued hen still lived on, and a warrior Rhode Island Red cockerel, a noble sire, a few feet north-west, was dead as a doornail . . .

He finished his brandy, saw them in his mind's eye for a

moment and set off along the windy pavements. He walked a mile or more without noticing; he was a good walker for all his bulk and belly, with the massive thighs and bulging calves of a colossus. People looked at him: the shoulders, the hard, leathered face. He didn't belong in the colourless amble of pavements, his urgency was a spiky aura travelling with him. He stopped to take his bearings: he had crossed Highbury Fields and now it was Blackstock Road, an untidy mess with the transient atmosphere of third-rate bazaars and pavement stalls of yams and sarees, Greek and Turkish eyes behind kebab windows: the days of draper and grocer, fathers and sons, serge suits, collars, ties, good mornings and evenings, were gone. Where was there a cobbler at his last, with awl, wax-end, heelball and a mouthful of tacks?

He bought half a bottle of brandy in a Pakistani self-service and waited for a bus to Stoke Newington. Duffy's bird lived in a road of substantial houses: three floors and basement of good red brick, a double door, fine windows unmarred by nets. Calnan had expected neglect, a nest of doorbells but there was a single button, polished and sedate as the other furnishings on the deep indigo surface. In the part-privacy of the embrasured porch he had a couple of tilts at the brandy bottle, arranged himself and rang. It was a solid deal eight-panelled door and no sound, not even of the bell, escaped from inside; but a safety-chain rattled and a handsome face – striking even, Calnan thought – forty-five, hardly that, smiled at him. Gold spectacles on a gold chain were worn like a pendant, her hands were pale and fine. Christ! he thought, a harbinger of death, where could he start? How?

'Good afternoon.' She smiled.

Duffy had struck it rich: her voice was deep and comforting, without a trace of impatience.

'We have,' he said, pausing to rush at it, 'a mutual friend, I think. My name is Calnan. I have the Trade Winds at Dalston,' he explained. 'A pub, that is.'

'Yes,' she said, understanding at once. 'You've often been mentioned.'

She opened the door. By God, Calnan thought, she was a beautiful woman and the hallway behind her had the palest of cream walls, and prints along it were little splashes of colour. They moved soundlessly on the carpet.

'I don't know where to begin,' Calnan said.

'I think I understand,' she said. 'I probably expected you at some time. Would you try a glass of port? Brandy, perhaps?'

'Port,' Calnan said. 'I hope you'll join me.'

'Well,' the smile was weaker now, 'just the tiniest measure. I'm not very good at drinking.'

He had been expected? Duffy, he pondered: perhaps she had been privy to some secret illness he nursed; but she was a thoroughbred; she knew what was in the pipeline but there would be no blubbering or squawking. Grief was a private thing. Calnan felt an immense gratitude. He tried to envision a midweek debauch, the winebibbery, the bottles, the swish of a silk robe against flesh, the smiles; but the colours failed, ran into a pool of surrealism.

He sat in the warm leather reassurance of a chesterfield armchair, large and spacious enough for his bulk. The port glass seemed brittle as egg-glaze.

'You've known him quite a while then?' he tried.

'Roderick?' she said. 'Oh yes, it must be two years since Roderick started visiting.'

Christ! Calnan thought: the publican's alarm system, sensitive as a cobweb, flashed at all points from brain to extremities. 'Roderick?' he said, nodding, and sipped his port.

'A great pride in his name. In his family too. I like that in a man. Threadbare times, even poverty, can arrive at any doorstep.'

Calnan, groping for a lifeline, raised his glass a fraction in agreement.

'A fine man,' she said. 'Roderick Hodder O'Callaghan

Davis. We call him Roddy. He likes that. What do his friends call him?'

The feedline came tantalisingly close to Calnan and passed him by. 'Oh, it had to be Roderick,' he said. 'He was an exact man. He didn't stand for short cuts.'

The change of tense confused her for a moment, but she brushed it aside, set forth to be at grips with distastefulness. The room had the kind of elegance that living bestows; a used room: a lot of precious things, an original painting or two, white bookshelves, hundreds of books; an inviting place and, through partly open doors, the table and sideboard of a dining room. He tried again to envisage 'Roddy' nosing the clarets, the burgundies, holding them longingly in the mouth before sending them to join and enhance the entrées and *pièces de résistance* of these set piece occasions. And on to silken robes!

'Did he give you my name?'

'No,' Calnan said.

'I didn't think he would. He's an honourable man.' She looked appraisingly at Calnan and hardly with approbation. 'My name is Mrs Lucinda Carter,' she announced. 'Did you have Roddy followed? And for such a pittance! Really, Mr Calnan!'

Calnan had a great pulsing desire to fill the room with raking blasts of profanity. He wondered in what lickspittle role he had been cast. But suddenly he was sobered at the thought of unpleasant duty still to be done; a dark cloud of confusion sat on his brain.

'I know about Roddy's indebtedness,' she said. 'Five hundred pounds you loaned him, wasn't it? On that sad occasion, the death of his father last year. He hasn't recovered from it, you know? He was, ironically, a favourite son. The prodigal of course, but loved.'

'I didn't know his father,' Calnan said.

'A veterinary of high reputation over there among Irish and expatriate gentry. He had once dreamed Roddy would follow in his footsteps.'

'The best laid schemes,' Calnan said. 'Did he leave a lot of money? His father, that is?'

'Yes.' She smiled with just a trace of pity towards Calnan. 'And Roddy, honour before all things, assigned his share to charity.'

'Ah,' Calnan said; he unashamedly took the brandy bottle from his pocket and drank deeply. She stared without comment. Calnan said, 'Five hundred pounds?'

'He gave you three. We insisted. We wanted so much to wipe it out in one fell swoop for him but he wouldn't hear of it.' She rang a wall bell, three pushes, a signal obviously, and in a few moments a tall austere man, remote, pale as precious napery, arrived. 'Idris,' she said, 'this is Roddy's creditor who causes him such anguish. That silly little two hundred pounds. A public house keeper from Dalston.'

At the arrival of this insubstantial ghostly man, Calnan hoisted himself from his chair. A *ménage à trois* whirled like a catherine wheel in his brain and he was staggered by permutations: all three joined in ecstasy, whips and piggybacks, cameras, switches, transvestite capers and cartwheels while the wine breathed and roast beef simmered in the kitchen.

'Roddy got in touch with our Rotary,' the man said. 'Dedicated to peace, you see. We admire him greatly and, of course, we always have a watchful eye for the once proud gentlefolk on whom misfortune sits most heavily. Roddy comes for lunch on Thursdays, a pleasant meal, and a little cash to tide him over.' He was at the writing desk now. 'I'll give you a cheque for two hundred.' He looked very hard at Calnan. 'And I want you to leave him alone.' He waved his pen. 'I don't have to do this, you see. Debts incurred in drinking dens are irredeemable, you know. He is a gifted man.'

'A hundred and eighty,' Calnan said. 'He was paying off at a pound a week when he had it.' Somehow he wanted to insulate them from street wisdom, the winter of Duffy's world, his own.

The Carters looked at each other with wistful smiles. 'You see?' they said simultaneously to Calnan.

Calnan nodded to preserve the dream.

'One hundred and eighty.' Mr Carter handed over the cheque.

Calnan arranged himself to leave. And now, this was the moment. 'Roddy,' he said, 'is dead.' He had almost said 'Duffy'.

The room was silent, not even the ticking of a clock; no children played in the Carters' road, not even traffic passed.

'Dead,' Mr Carter stated eventually, as if ruling off a cherished account. 'Oh dear!' Lucinda said. 'The air was troubled last night. We felt it.'

'Let me have particulars,' Mr Carter said briskly. 'We'll see to funeral arrangements of course. He had no living kith or kin.'

'The funeral is paid for,' Calnan said. 'He had a host of admirers, you see. The arrangements are being made, I'll telephone you.'

Mr Carter gave him his card. They came to the doorstep with him. 'I'm sorry if I seem abrupt . . . I didn't quite get your name . . .'

'Calnan.'

'As I said, I'm sorry if I seem abrupt, Calnan. But money grubbing at a time like this is distasteful. There would have been more decorum in waiting until he had been laid to rest. Good day to you.'

At the end of the hallway, doors lay open to a conservatory of foliage and tinted glass; an oak table, round, beautiful, unpolished; a trace of incense, Calnan thought. The floor was a shaded board of marquetry: suns and moons and symbols in place about a brilliant white pentagram.

Calnan nodded; he could see his reflection in the deep, deep blue of the street door as it snapped shut.

When he was out of sight he tore Mr Carter's cheque into small pieces and released them on the next gust of wind that rushed at him across Stoke Newington Common. He drank more brandy and looked at his watch.

Time to get back.

A dog, a forepaw raised delicately, limped on three feet to a basement gate. Duffy, veterinary surgeon, he thought: lame and halting dogs gathered about him.

He found himself, strangely, in good humour again, overpowered, he thought, with the absurdity of the day: Lucinda brave at the passing over of Roderick Hodder O'Callaghan Davis; Idris giving death its decorum; dodger Duffy dead in Highgate and how many *doppelgängers* with him? And the incense, Calnan thought: the air had been troubled last night.

4

*H*e walked with great pushing strides down the narrow alleys off Kingsland: the brandy was coursing now and he breathed deeply in and exhaled, feeling the lightness of himself and his distance from the world. The wind was rising and, like a tumbleweed, an empty beer can was blown past, clattering on and on until he dismissed it; rags and wrappers and hosts of dust, in a pattern of Keystone Cops, rushed to intersections and spun and whirled and vanished. There was a phone booth without a single pane of glass intact, urine drying on the floor. The wind whistled through it. He rang Morgan. A church tower clock, God help it, pealed the hour of six; and it was already dark.

'I'm sorry,' he told Morgan. 'There was a journey to make. A few journeys. Duffy-work. Look after yourself. Get your help in. And Taff? My decorators? Propped against the fire, are they?'

'Yes,' Morgan said.

'Ears cocked?'

'I'd say.'

'Finished at five?'

Morgan laughed.

'Beer on the nod?'

'That's it.'

'They're good for twenty-five,' Calnan said. 'And watch for tricks.'

'I will.'

'Maybe I'll get there soon.'

He hung up and looked at his feet planted in the urine, the red geometric skeleton of the phone booth built around him; the wind was beginning to chill his legs and the small of his back.

It was a long narrow street of emptiness, two-up-two-down houses on one side, vacant, nailed and boarded, awaiting the dozer and the ball-crane; and he squinted through the wind at the blind towering windows of an abandoned estate that fouled the opposite side; three, four acres of stacked, tenantless warrens hardly twenty years old, empty as if a grimy voracious plague had swept through them. He stood and listened in the wind for the distant sound of traffic. Behind the choked highways of an evening rush forgotten voids like this existed: a fault in a casting, a knot-hole, a vacuum, someplace outside the stream of time, dead as an old picture. He went on past the empty condemned dwellings where once there had been a stir and smells of food and children; and midwives pedalling by on indestructible cycles. He flung his feet out and heard them beat on the flagged pavements. Jesus, he thought, whatever plague had struck had killed not a few streets or alleys but a whole microcosmic world of friends and foes, with a shop window or a stall for every need until the hearse did its final lap of honour and vanished. A churchyard was an overgrown acre of shrubs gone wild, stones and effigies toppled and vandalised behind iron railings and gates that inexplicably had been missed by the hawks and armourers of war years. He leant his weight against the gate, sunk it further into the turf and weeds and dumped refuse. It groaned at him and the clock struck the quarter. He looked up at the lantern spire in the growing darkness: the gold-leafed clock hands and Roman numerals still had a dim glimmer of importance, surveying even such desolation: a decapitated Christ child, drunken slabs of marble, stones, gravemarkers, and a wounded angel, single-winged, forlorn. For a moment he thought of Duffy on his cold slab in

Highgate, awaiting the mortuary apprentices and the perusal of his contents. 'Repeat the dose,' Duffy would orate: 'A bird never flew on one wing.' Or an angel, Calnan thought, looking at the gentle marble face and joined hands. And all the gulps and groans, he thought, the grief that had ringed each corpse-plot for as long only as the gold-leafed hands took to span a quadrant.

The church doors were bolted, chained against God and man: mullioned panels, rusting symmetrical hinges and whorls and extravagance. Calnan sat on the doorstep and drank from his brandy bottle. The wind rushed and jigged in the shrubs, in the tall weeds and grass — filled his mind with sound.

A grey blob rose up out of the basement steps beside him and, as if suddenly inflated, became an old smiling man. He wore a long overcoat and his threadlike hair was frantic in the wind.

'Are you waiting to get in?' he asked Calnan. 'It's been closed for twenty years.'

'I have great patience,' Calnan said.

The little man laughed. 'I wind the clock,' he said as if it were as commonplace as bus-driving. 'A beautiful sound, isn't it? Did you hear?'

'Yes.'

He looked up. 'Even more beautiful up there, you see. With the wind and echoes on the stone stairs. Very beautiful.'

'Yes.'

'Who did you think wound it?' he shot at Calnan like a party riddle.

'God, I suppose,' Calnan said with a bark of amusement and the little man's laughter, treble enough to shatter glass, took off on the wind.

'I'm sixty-eight years winding it,' he said. 'A family job really. Three generations.' He nodded at a ruptured vault slab, the gravestones falling in battle, the huge overgrown mouth of nature in the act of swallowing. 'Only the nobs had

43

churchyard plots like this, you see. Special. Very big people under our feet here. Money. The vault's a jeweller,' he pointed. 'And there's a judge, and a doctor there. Big men with big shops too. A lot of them. Money everywhere. And the angel, sad isn't it? Freshest of graves too.'

Calnan wondered.

'The last ground opened, you see. A war grave you could call it, I suppose. Subaltern, nineteen years. It's on the stone. Heir to the manor far as you'll walk. Not this last war, mind. The one before.' He stood and pondered. 'No, I tell a lie. The one before that. South Africa, it was. They brought him back, the parents, and then followed him down the hole in a year. They're all down there. Three of them. Funny, isn't it?'

'Hilarious,' Calnan said.

The little man wandered away, nodding his head at perhaps the mad humour of the world or the oddity of Calnan.

Calnan drank again and looked at the grounded angel. The little man waved, unseen, from the gate and was gone.

Some exposed thread of memory reminded Calnan of glossy American god-magazines: sunbursts and the unblemished, untrammelled face of virtuous youth. They came to him from Sacramento with, sometimes, brief words of wisdom penned on the margin or with perhaps an interposed card at Christmas time. 'Many a life has been changed by reading just one holy book,' he remembered; or 'I pray for you every day. Pray for me sometimes – Stephen.'

Stephen: he could scarcely remember him and, if at all, with a flicker of impatience: a priest, how many years in Sacramento and its environs, sure that in London, England, was his errant sibling, a ponce, a brothel keeper, a publican. Once it had been written: 'I still have my Irish accent. I hope you have yours.'

Oh God, Calnan thought. He leant back against the stout pillars of the portico, remembered dirt roads and streams and hand-me-down clouts; buses to Dublin on tarmac highways, railway stations, boats, sickness, sitting in the wind: they became for him almost sonar images in a limitless echo chamber . . .

When he awoke he was chilled to the bone. The wind had dropped hardly at all but the sleety flecks of rain in it had roused him. He saw the virginal face of the marble angel beyond the reach of human pain or death. Christ! the cold! he thought. His teeth chattered, his pulse was pounding again and he frantically dragged out the brandy bottle, unscrewed the cap that slipped in his spastic fingers. He drained the brandy, paused. His bladder ached for release. He stood up in the intense darkness now. How long, he wondered, and clasping his hands, focused the watch-face on his wrist. After nine o'clock! He steadied himself, gathering great breaths, and steered a course between clumps and stones to the nearest shrub: it came to his chin, a speckled laurel bush, and as he peered out over it he released his powerful deluge of water. He closed his eyes and groaned his relief. Then suddenly there was the shrill scream of a woman, whipped past on the wind like train passing train: his whole body jerked, the wind caught him and urine sprayed across his trousers and shoes. He roared like something wounded.

The clock pealed another quarter.

When he had arranged himself, resigned himself to discomfort, and picked his steps out to the pavement, two policemen, not more than schoolboys, hidden at the gate pillars, pounced on him. One had his shoulders, the other faced him in death-defying resolve, still sending out crisp radio messages of progress to base. 'Innocent,' Calnan said humorously to the humourless. A squad car came and whisked them away. Hardly a block. It passed nine thirty-one on the sweatroom clock while they awaited the arrival of an overweight sergeant. Very nasty, Calnan decided, when he arrived: greasy, mean, ill maybe.

'This him?' he asked the young falcons.

They nodded.

'Pissin' on graves, was you?' he said almost happily to Calnan.

'Pissin' in a bush,' Calnan said.

'In a bush, was it now?' he said in a horrendous mimicry of Calnan. 'A Mick, bejasus, to round it off! Pissin' Irish piss on consecrated ground, you filthy bastard!' The two young men stood in wonder at the expertise of interrogation. 'Details!' he snapped at one of them who consulted his notebook.

'Nine fifteen, sir, in Sebastopol Street, I became aware of female screams which I would describe as terror stricken. I mentioned same to Constable Perkins who agreed . . .'

'Molested, was she?'

'No, sir. At least no complaint was lodged. She was on her way to bingo. Coloured lady. A short cut, she explained. Then, in very frightened tones, she stated: "I–think–I–seen–a–ghost."'

'A ghost?'

'Well, it transpired, sir, it was the detained person's head. He was urinating in the churchyard of St James's, behind a bush, and to a female person of nervous disposition, proceeding through a demolition area, it seemed as if the head might be floating in the air. Constable Perkins and I were a little startled at first, sir.'

The sergeant nodded. 'A nice bloody turnip to see floating in the air. You like graveyards, do you?' he said in a kind of whispered confidence to Calnan.

Calnan thought of the vinegar of week-old beer.

'Offered his name as Robert Emmet Calnan of Dalston Junction and declined to give further information.' The notebooked constable was grave as a Puritan but for a moment he drained away just the palest degree of formality from his voice, to add: 'It could be mooted, sir, that the forenames Robert Emmet, are provocative, politically undesirable, that is. A terrorist of the last century over there,' he explained. 'Duly apprehended, convicted and hanged, of course.' He smiled in bleak apology of his erudition. 'I'm taking a degree, sir. I thought the association might be pertinent.'

'Mmmm.' The sergeant appraised him with the birth of caution. And then to Calnan, 'So you like graveyards?'

'They must be visited from time to time.'

'Must they? A compulsion, Pat? You have a mission, is that it? Suddenly a great urge to be in a graveyard, and you're off! And when you get there?' He smiled encouragingly to Calnan. 'Bones, skulls, maybe? I'll bet you know a vault here and there with a door that'll push in before your big belly, and you can slide back the lids of coffins and see what's left? Exciting, Pat?' He turned and studied his constables again. 'You're sure he was urinating? Not something else?'

There was silence. 'Until he reached us at the pavement the precise functions of his hands were unknown to us,' the history man said.

'Ah!' The sergeant pondered in exposition of the bizarre. 'The seeds of life on the dust of death, you understand?'

Calnan looked at the pale green walls, the lino-tiled floor, the table where he and this vicarious grave-plunderer confronted each other. The constables stood by the door. There was no window. Nothing else. Bareness.

'What journeys did you make today?' the sergeant asked him gently. Calnan considered for a moment and relished just an instant dream of putting a fist on the greasy head before him, hammering him, like a nail, into the flooring. But there lay the road to disaster. To tell him of Duffy's corpse and the Clincher's reverence with peppermint and girly books in Upper Street would shoot him into a frenzied necrophiliac orbit that might end anywhere.

'I like to walk,' Calnan said.

'All day?'

'Sometimes. A drink here and there, of course.'

'Where?'

'Pubs I can never remember.' Calnan focused both his eyes

47

on one of the sergeant's. 'I don't like bones or skulls or desecration of churchyards.'

'Urinating on sacred places?' the bright young man posited.

'But was I?' Calnan said with a sudden attack. 'Or waving my knob at gravestones? Or what else? I'm a busy man.' He looked hard at the sergeant. 'Make your mind up!'

Silence fell on them. Somewhere in a distant room teacups rattled and there was laughter. The sergeant wrestled with his impatience. 'Don't leave yet, Pat. You're a bag of tricks. A one-man show. Now, what would take a man, in winter wind, in darkness, into a churchyard?'

'To wind the clock, maybe,' Calnan said. He stood. 'Ring the nick at Dalston. The Trade Winds, tell them. I keep open house for cops and robbers. Even little presents to the nick at Christmas. I'm a publican.'

The less gifted constable was sent to check; the sergeant's eyes planned a retreat; the historian was frantic for blood: he said, 'You must be proud of a name like Robert Emmet?'

Calnan didn't reply to questions like that.

'Parents passing the holy message, could it be?'

Calnan thought of brandy and the warmth of his red room, the chain of juggernauts coming up from the docks. The noise would be music.

'Are you a member of an organisation, Mr Calnan?'

Calnan nodded. 'The LVA.'

The sergeant was still as the marble angel; the historian worked at it.

'The Licensed Victuallers' Association,' Calnan said sadly. 'A band of ageing tosspots.'

'I'll check you out myself,' the sergeant barked for an exit line; and when the door closed behind him, the history man was suddenly bereft, at a loss.

'The Trade Winds at Dalston,' Calnan told him. 'Some night you're free come in for a piss. If you can't find a churchyard handy. A pity,' he said, 'my sconce wasn't black as the black mare that screeched at me.'

The historian's face twitched, teetered on the brink of some doubtful emotion. The dull one returned. 'You can go,' he said with a creditable display of urbanity. 'The sergeant says, shift, move!' He escorted Calnan to the street. 'You're a clever spud, aren't you?' he said. 'I'll keep an eye on you and the Trade Winds, shithead.'

'You'll go far,' Calnan told him. 'You won't need history.'

He walked more than a mile to the High Road before he caught a cab to Dalston. Cassie's Metro was gone, he noted, on errands of mercy and manipulation for the less unfortunate. The Trade Winds was alive: heat, smoke, a wavering shout of conversation enveloped him like a spouse as he pushed in the swing-doors; his name was called out everywhere so that, in the style of some proletarian despot, he smiled at no one in particular, raised a hand in salutation as he moved.

Morgan, in full flow, covered the ring of the bar, smooth, effortless, on ice; his helpers, smart as paint, Blondie and Sher, in flimsy skirts and tops, hard as nails, could giggle laughter, shout or spit, outswear a navvy. Calnan nodded; they smiled and winked. Morgan brought a measure of brandy, a glass of beer.

'Brisk.'

'Ticking over, guv'nor.' Morgan moved away, smoothing Blondie's bottom as he went. She smiled.

Brandy had no taste now, only shock and warmth; the beer was cold as the churchyard. He drained the glasses and with the same mask of *bonhomie* pushed to his private doorway and up the stairs of the morningtime sweat to his red room and a moment's peace.

The bed, hardly ever dressed or arranged, the bedside table, the pale remnants of the brandy bottle, stood still in time. How long since he had sweated and the phone had rung endlessly? Eighteen, nineteen hours, he thought. The noise from the bar filtered up to him now and tobacco smoke, hardly visible, filled every corner and cranny. Neelan and Mackessy, ignored by him, had holla-ed across the crowd,

49

but they'd want to wait to drink the balance of their sub and borrow again and doss. He went to the bedside table, to the brandy bottle, sipped its flatness and knew they had gulped it and topped it with water. He smiled a stab of irritation. It was good to be home in the red room, somehow safe, he thought. It was turned half-past ten. The tossed bed was calling for him but he turned his back on it, kept in motion.

He went to the bathroom to gaze on the work in progress of his flawed contractors, his artists: naked joists of ceiling ready for plasterboard, great tumescences of sagging walls excised and filled; the floor, the discoloured bath, a carpet of detritus unswept: broken lath, horsehair, plaster. The smell of age.

Mackessy and Neelan: he had a moment's compassion for them, just a moment; chancers, con-men, thieves: all the attributes for survival in alien seas were there. Duffy's death was the close encounter, the rabbit punch to test them, and they were fighting back with brandy and bitter to keep death and oblivion at a distance, to carry on like heroes from moment to moment. That was every day for all of them.

The handbasin was clean; he poured the water hot and steaming, cupped it up in huge handfuls against his face, scrubbed his hands and nails; and then, cold water on his skin until he could hardly bear it. The towel on his face and closed eyes was soft as down. He smiled encouragingly at himself in the mirror, arranged his tie, his hair, his whole posture, as if part of some blind psychological panacea for the forgotten, the desolate. And then his smile faded and he remembered the sergeant. 'A nice bloody turnip to see floating in the air.' Sick surgeons, frayed fuzz, clowns weeping at the absence of laughter; a place for them all. He remembered the silent, brooding, young bull who would have the Trade Winds in his surveillance. There was a little moment of anger and uneasiness.

He went downstairs into the milling roar of Friday night escape and found Mackessy in high key awaiting him, ready to part the seas for him, to guide him to a stool; and Neelan, holding his drunkenness with an old expertise, a ball-point poised over sheets of paper: an image from some crazed canvas of an arrogant baron flouting his literacy. One of their retinue was buying drinks and, in a kind of shouting whisper, Mackessy reminded him that the guv'nor's shot was 'cognac'.

'That's brandy,' Neelan explained. 'A double brandy, of course, my darling,' he amended in an awful groping kindness.

The tall long-legged Blondie with earrings and swishing hair, smiled at him with her teeth.

'And one for yourself. Your pleasure,' Neelan added with the carelessness of a prodigal, a helpless broadcaster of largesse.

Calnan sat and looked at the ball-point poised like a precious fag-holder of the roaring twenties, and heavy sheets of foolscap paper on a makeshift clipboard, each headed with some freakish splash of design and calligraphy. He sipped at the brandy, caught a flicker of Morgan's eye. Neelan suddenly, in sinner's humility before his pontiff, proffered the foolscap sheets for approval. In a pencilled jungle of curves and curlicues, like a tangled skein of flimsy cotton, Calnan could decipher, *In Memoriam James Duffy*. There was even a harp and a cluster of shamrocks sprouting magically from so murderous a jungle of undergrowth.

'A round tower would have been nice,' Calnan said.

'I was caught for space,' Neelan explained. 'The round tower, of course, and the sleeping wolfhound are part of our heritage. But they need room. I did my best.'

'You did,' Calnan said.

A quatrain of verse sat over the ruled columns that were designated 'name', 'address', 'offering'. It was a funeral collection for Duffy.

'Offering?' Calnan said. 'Do you think they'll stand for that?'

'We can explain it,' Mackessy said. 'If necessary. It's a generous word.'

'Duffy's whip!' Neelan said. 'That'll be the password.' He dismissed the difficulty. 'Read the poetry, Cal. Just a little thing I knocked up for the occasion, you understand. Listen! Listen!' He silenced the immediate circle. 'The guv'nor will read us the verse.'

Calnan looked at him in a moment of brooding intent.

'Order for the guv'nor,' Mackessy said with quiet dignity. Morgan was poker-faced at the till.

'Listen to this, my jewel,' Neelan said to Sher, the ginger barmaid and she paused in her hurry and waited in red pouted impatience.

Calnan read tonelessly:

> '"Good night," he said, "I'll see you, lads."
> A smile, a laugh, a nod.
> But Death was waiting in the wings,
> To take him back to God.'

Calnan groaned in his thoughts: he saw Duffy in flight from some strange paradisiac reformatory, a ticket-of-leave man, dragged back to the feet of God, remission lost. A few moments of ostensibly stunned silence were preserved within the little circle while the evening thundered on.

'I had no idea you could write poetry like that, guv'nor,' someone said to Calnan out of the hush and there was a little flutter of handclaps from faceless sycophants, and nodding exchanges of approbation.

'Who constructed this?' Calnan said, loud enough to make silence and lay blame where it belonged.

'I did!' Neelan was savage for recognition; the colour crept back to his face. 'The guv'nor has honoured us with his rendering. The reading of poetry is an art and we have been privileged this evening, gentlemen.'

Neelan's face glistened in a smoky aura of hubris; he raised his glass perfunctorily to Calnan. 'I don't have much time,' he was explaining to the vulgus. 'Poetry takes time, you see. Concentrated, pure, like a shot of Drambuie. I had a piece in the paper once in my schooldays. I have it somewhere in the digs. I must bring it in some night.'

'Let me know,' Calnan said. 'I'll be here to read it for you.'

Mackessy, displaced by such literary effulgence, grabbed the foolscap sheets. 'There's work to be done,' he said. 'The opening of Duffy's whip, God rest him. Would you do us the honour, Cal?'

Neelan stood now, with clipboard and pen, like a book-maker's clerk; and Mackessy, with an empty shoe-box, announced: 'Name . . . the guv'nor! . . . Got that?'

Neelan recorded, flourished the ball-point. 'Done!'

'The honour of opening the proceedings goes to the guv'nor, of course,' Mackessy explained as if to restrain the restrained.

'Offering?' Neelan chimed.

'Make it substantial,' Mackessy said quietly in Calnan's ear. 'It sets the pace. There's a lot of mean bastards wouldn't give you a fag-end. Twenty will be fine. No more than that, mind! No need to overdo it.'

'Offering?' Neelan chimed out once again.

Calnan leant over to Neelan and whispered. 'If you say that again I'll beat your brains out with the clipboard.'

'Twenty pounds from the guv'nor,' Mackessy announced.

'Twenty pounds,' Neelan echoed and gravely entered it.

Mackessy held out the box, said in hushed confidence again, 'Put a twenty in the box, Cal. A twenty looking up at them is a great spur.'

'For what?' Calnan said. 'Robbery with violence? Move yourself! It's a quarter to the bell. Move, get your finger out! And that bathroom up there is a bombed-site!'

Mackessy retreated with grace, showed a smiling face to the world; Neelan, his clerk, followed behind. Calnan drank, exchanged the ghost of a smile with Morgan, shut himself away from the evening.

The cabinet lights, the window lanterns, the counter lights, flicked out; wet towels hung across the pumps; the day was done. Morgan, disarming as a smiling villain, sang out the parting jingles. '. . . Now gents, leave your glasses, shift your asses . . . hurry, hurry, hurry! We open every day . . . we never go away . . . hurry now my lovelies!'

Passing Calnan, he said, 'Yours is on the sideboard, guv'nor.' He moved away, deep into the crowd.

Calnan stood. It was Morgan's nod that, up there, the collected notes of the day were under his pillow; and brandy beside them. In half an hour the bar would be silent, glasses washed, ashtrays tipped, tables and counters swabbed; in the cellar, spillage, slops, waste for resale would be filtering into a violated keg; a jug set aside for the morning and dying Jock. Taff knew the tricks: a drink or two with his lassies and, maybe, hold one back for a tumble on the carpet.

Calnan escaped through the crowd, climbed the stairs to his red room, undressed to his underclothes and got between the coarseness of the blankets. He felt for the money and the brandy bottle beneath the pillow, listened to the traffic somehow friendly tonight: a godsent weariness, a long awaited anodyne came down to him.

An hour later, more perhaps, he surfaced for a moment or two; he heard the street door below snap shut, the rattle of keys, the click of the lock, the scrape and crash of metal as Taff struggled with ageing tumblers, and the keys again as they clattered on the pavement: laughter, profanity. Blondie's tinkling giggle. The room was full of strange tender comfort as he drifted away.

5

The sound of the till, the sharp spear of its bell, the slam of the drawer awakened Calnan. He thought about it. A woolly murmur of voices; laughter, distant laughter that he might have heard before, and then the ring-slam of the till again. He sat up. It was always night-time in his room, an endless cycle of faintly red hours. It might be any time. The sound of the traffic was smaller. He tried to focus his wrist-watch but the face, the hands, the numerals were shifting, spoiled like a speed-blur on an old snapshot.

Confusion spurred him; he was afraid of it. To stand, to feel the floor gritty with dust beneath him, to move, all for a moment were beyond his power as if he had awakened with only his groping mind alive in a stricken body. He heaved himself out of a nightmare, it seemed, into mobility and trotted the dozen or so paces to the bathroom. The naked joists, the walls, the carpet of ancient rubbish, reassured him with their ugliness. He glanced in the mirror at his own tortured eyes, the oily pain in them. A key hung about his neck like a crucifix. The time! he thought. And then suddenly he was rushing back to the bedroom to push aside the damp pillow. The notes were there! He locked them in the safe and rested. The time! Jesus, it was almost two o'clock, daylight near spent! He had drowsed, lain awake, for each hour until dawn and then, unbelievably, slept like the dead; his bladder was a bar of pain across his groin.

He had emptied himself and shaved and dressed to the kind of sober respectability that he liked to think was unremarkable, when he thought of the brandy bottle. He was pleased about it: he examined his almost dry hands and fingers – a little unsteady but without a twitch. It might be a good day with a need only for a moderate infusion of alcohol: there were good days and bad days. He remembered the long haul of yesterday and the load he had carried and, as he descended the stairs, he remembered the greasy sergeant in the sweat-room: a turnip-head, was Paddy; and the Carters of Stoke Newington, patrons of Roderick Hodder O'Callaghan Davis, had been a little sickened at his unforgivable greed in the face of death. Roderick Hodder O'Callaghan Davis! He dug in his breast pocket for Carter's number and climbed the stairs again. He rang the Clincher at the Chapels of Rest.

'The name on the coffin plate will be Roderick Hodder O'Callaghan Davis,' he told him.

'On that fellow Duffy's coffin?'

'That's right,' Calnan said. 'He was a dodgy spiritualist too, I think.'

'By God!' the Clincher said, cracking his sanctimonious shell.

'And listen,' Calnan said: he gave him Carter's phone number. 'Send details of Roderick Hodder O'Callaghan Davis's cremation and run wild on all that courtesy and reverence thing.'

'Listen Cal . . .'

'And I owe you.'

Calnan took a little brandy and went downstairs. The television was on: out of a foggy racecourse somewhere horses jumped at him. The bar was well peopled; Morgan and Blondie were on a brisk run. Christ, it was Saturday! he was suddenly aware. A man should always know what day of the week it was, he thought. He made a gesture of hopelessness to Morgan. 'Keep it going,' he told him.

'Beer?'

Calnan nodded. 'Duffy's name is Davis now. Roderick Davis.'

In the mirror above the till he could see Neelan and Mackessy, unaware, still assessing some plan of campaign as they approached, a black aura of mischief surrounding them. But when they stood on either side of him a warmth of affection and camaraderie came with them, with the speed of a spray can.

Before they settled Calnan struck. 'Going to make a start? Good.'

'A start?' Mackessy said, making allowance for yesterday's inroads and the still bemused state of Calnan's brainbox.

'The bathroom,' Calnan said, 'I'd need to be a steeplejack to relieve myself. You must have escaped before the ceiling came down.'

'You have the advantage of us,' Neelan said, barely smiling, coping with the disabled, the handicapped.

'There's two cubic yards of muck on the floor,' Calnan said. They were drinking brandy, he noted.

Mackessy downed his measure and the tap of his glass on the counter was a signal of annoyance, disbelief.

'Suffering God!' It was Neelan gathering his disgust like phlegm.

'Brennan!' Mackessy whispered. 'Did he not do it? The cleaning?'

'Look,' Calnan said, 'I don't want to make a production of it. I'm not in the mood for play-acting.'

'Brennan!' Neelan hissed at him. 'The smudger, Brennan!'

'We gave him a pound,' Mackessy spelt it out. 'A pound!'

'To clear the muck, the rubbish. We put a pound in his hand. Three hours ago!' A pound might have been some limitless bill of exchange.

'You subcontracted the groundwork,' Calnan said. 'Site clearance by Brennan. Christ, I overpriced the job!'

'Be fair now,' Mackessy said with a kind of patently false humility that could upset Calnan. 'We sweated like dogs there

57

yesterday in dust a hundred years old and as fine as powder. It nearly took a jack-hammer to clear my nose.'

'We came out of it with flour-bag faces, a couple of sick mummers,' Neelan said, 'and burnt holes for eyes and mouths.' He tossed back his brandy at the unpleasantness remembered, scanned the drinkers for Brennan's foxy head. 'Where did he get to?'

'Today is Saturday,' Calnan said.

'That's right,' Mackessy said indulgently.

'Market day.'

Neelan tapped the counter, Mackessy nodded: they brooded, shrugged away the oversight. Saturday!

Saturday, it was Brennan's joy to traipse the huge endless labyrinth of street market on the High Road, obsessed with the beauty of the discarded, the flawed, the rubbish; some ancient atavistic gene filled his mind with commercial power and grandeur.

'What plans for today?' Calnan asked.

There was a silence and Mackessy, shaking himself back to reality, apologised. 'I was miles away. That flip-flop Brennan flashing our pound round the market is a bit more than a liberty.' He ordered brandy for Neelan and himself. Morgan, poker-faced, came and went.

'Leave my drinking to me,' Calnan told them. 'What about today?'

'Today is Saturday,' Neelan said.

Calnan nodded. 'I think we can agree on that.'

'We never do more than five days,' Mackessy said in disbelief at Calnan's unawareness of trades law.

'What five days?' Calnan asked.

'Saturday and Sunday are the working man's weekend!' Neelan stated with a smiling sharpness. 'A few hours of social activity, an escape from the clock.' He shook his head in mild reprimand. 'The twentieth century, Cal!'

'Twentieth century my arse!' Calnan said. 'No work, no pay.'

'Cal, Cal!' Mackessy, the honest peacemaker, said. 'Have a drink.'

'No drink.'

'These are not pleasant days, you'll agree. Duffy stiff as a board and a period of readjustment ahead for all of us. Try to bear with us, Cal. We can't brave the bullet like the warrior born. But I'll state a fact for you; when that bathroom is finished it'll be a showpiece.' He looked to Neelan.

'A showpiece,' Neelan confirmed. 'And when Brennan drags himself back from the market he'll earn his pound. Not my style to leave dirty work behind me. You'll have to excuse us now,' he said brusquely. 'Half-past two.'

Mackessy nodded with funereal significance, fixing triviality in its place. He called to Morgan for clipboard and shoe-box. 'Duffy's whip,' he explained to Calnan. 'We'll take a few bob now. A fair night last night. Of course Duffy was a popular man.' He held up the empty box. 'With another round tonight and a push tomorrow lunchtime, it'll put a smile on Duffy's face, wherever he is.'

'On the slab,' Calnan said. 'They're having a look inside him this morning.'

'Don't talk about it!' Neelan stood, head bowed, eyes closed in horror.

'The flowers are on order,' Mackessy said.

The shoe-box empty, the clipboard bare, Calnan noted; he watched Mackessy prime the box with a fiver; Neelan produced the sub-sheets from his innermost pocket and they were already on their mission. There was a great excess of zeal, care and security, Calnan thought.

'They took a pot of money last night,' Morgan said quietly. 'A ton and a half, maybe more.'

'The cash? Who's the banker?'

'Half and half. A mutual trust. Splits the risk, Neelan says.'

'Or doubles it? You didn't give anything?'

'Christ!' Morgan said.

Calnan laughed silently, without expression, his body

shaking a little. 'Keep an eye,' he said.

Leggy Blondie passed and smiled at Calnan. Morgan looked after her. 'A nice little machine,' he said.

Closed Saturday afternoon doors, blind windows of pubs, somehow remarkable in High Street turmoil and forgotten in back doubles, were a sham: the hooked, the forlorn, the lickerish, sat on in a warmth of alcohol where syllables became important, and there was so much to be said, and tomorrow was Sunday. The Law, more sensible than the lawmakers, went about other business.

The doors of the Trade Winds shut; Brennan fresh from the market world, put on his potman's hat, did enough with ashtrays and tables to keep untidiness at bay. Blondie took over; Morgan seemed to have vanished, gone for an hour or two to his doll's house where Sher might minister to him. And Mackessy and Neelan were tireless mendicants.

'A lively market down there today.' Brennan paused for a break. 'Lively for late November, you'd say, but you forget Christmas is on the home stretch.' Philosophy froze him motionless for a moment. 'When you and I, Cal, are sunbathing they're on to jingle bells and paperchains. Always on the ball, market people. You know something?' He gazed solemnly at Calnan. 'I'm tempted sometimes to have a go myself. No push-over to get a licence of course. But I have my contacts.'

'What would you sell?' Calnan asked.

'Anything can be sold in the market from odd socks to bicycle chains.'

'Cleaning materials,' Calnan said. 'You'd be fairly expert on that.'

'You know,' Brennan said, 'that never struck me! Brushes, metal polish, the treatment of pewter, care of copper and glass . . .'

'Carpet shampoo,' Calnan said, 'toilet freshness. You could manage a little brochure, maybe?'

'I know a printer in Shoreditch.'

'"The Licensees' Guide to Health, Hygiene and Happiness".'

'You could've put me on to something there, Cal. I must think about it, do a bit of costing, you understand? People rushing at things tend to overreach themselves. I never do that.'

'I know,' Calnan said.

Brennan shot forward both his hands, showing three watches on each wrist. 'A few nice models this weekend.'

In the market, some trading agreement of honour existed between Brennan and a shifty Latvian of ill repute who pitched his second-time-round watch and clock emporium on the market pavements every Saturday: pushing watches on commission a half-a-mile from base seemed to clothe Brennan in the garb of international salesman and entrepreneur.

'Nothing over a fiver there.'

'I told you not to flog those arsehole things in the bar,' Calnan said in a moment of anger. 'People ring me up, sometimes in the middle of the night, and tell me their watch is stopped. I was threatened last week.'

Brennan moved off in wounded perplexity. Blondie smiled at Calnan again; the pace of drinking was slower now and steady behind closed doors, spaced with conversation, and she could cope without Morgan's power. For Mackessy she converted the shoe-box takings into fives, singles, odd change. He put the notes carefully in his pocket, looked critically at the odd coin and flung it in the box as a handsel for the evening appeal; Neelan, with the old-time expertise of an accountant, ran a finger down his page as if casting at electronic speed. A word or two passed between them and there was a nodding of heads: obviously a financial venture of exactitude and satisfaction. Cognac was purchased, Blondie was treated, Calnan eyed them without emotion, rebuffed hospitality. 'Buy your own,' he told them. 'You're dipping in the whip, aren't you?'

'Temporarily,' Neelan said with the kind of abruptness

reserved for people of property and commercial greed. 'By tomorrow lunch we'll have pushed four collections. Brain work and leg work, of course, but a willing gesture for a friend.'

Calnan nodded at the brandy. 'You'll be fifty quid short.'

Mackessy raised a hand for silence and peace, even admonished Neelan a trifle with a warning index finger. He said to Calnan, 'You're right, Cal. Yesterday was a tough session, a feed of drink, and by God we couldn't face the dust and smell of plaster and gloss this morning. There has to be a breathing space.' He seemed to think and calculate, let his heavy lids dip for a moment. 'There's three, four days of heavy weather out there in front of us. We're skint. Fifty won't touch it. A ton, maybe.'

Neelan, penitent now, nodded apology to Calnan, acknowledged in some slight degree his own shamefulness.

'I'm sorry, Cal,' he said. 'I'm still in a state of shock. I was out of order.'

Mackessy said, with the credibility of Grosvenor Place, 'Cal understands.' He allowed an adequate period of silence and then, as if in deliberate punishment of himself, screwed, pulled and tugged at a cheap Claddagh ring on his little finger. It was finally freed.

He placed it before Calnan. 'My mother's ring, Cal,' he said.

Calnan sensed, if not minor defeat, only the hollowest of victories.

'My mother's ring that'll go to the grave with me. May the Man above strike me down if I'd cast disrespect on it.' He pushed it closer to Calnan. 'Hold it, Cal,' he said, 'as a pledge of bounden duty to meet all debts and commitments at this sad time.'

There was silence: they held Calnan's humanity on a thread over a black hole of space.

'Pull us out,' Neelan whispered. 'Pay us for the job in advance.'

Mackessy said, 'I won't rest until that ring is back on my finger.'

Calnan was adjusting strategy. 'And the bathroom, the showpiece?' Some pride and principle must seem to be salvaged; seconds must tick away: the tensions and signs of inner struggle. He pushed the ring slowly back along the counter to Mackessy.

'Fifty,' he said. 'The balance when the job's done.'

Great false explosions of gratitude, overpowering, were distasteful to Calnan. He seemed to display a little anger at his own 'weakness'. He gave Mackessy five tens.

Neelan said, 'A man in a million, Cal! You still owe the whip twenty, of course,' he was forced to add with apparently great difficulty, his whole mien an expression of hatred of himself. 'But there's no hurry with it! None at all!'

Calnan pushed twenty across to him and listened to the bar-talk, rising and falling, like a wave over shingle, and the pause of undertow. A couple of young anglers, loaded with gear, finished their pints, anxious to be away: the thunder and fading roar of motor cycles was like the hysteria of runaway felons. They would sit, at optimum distances apart, on folding stools, at muddy polluted streams or subdued reservoirs, and open cans of homegrown maggots and gaze and listen; and glance sometimes at an infinity of stools and frozen stoics spread out like a broken worry beads. He remembered his bare feet on the wet grass after rain, the roaring and whirls of a flood river: a sally branch, a piece of string, a hook, a worm from the earth, trout hauled in and threaded on a stick or a loop of wire. The only man in the world . . .

'Hey!' He heard Neelan shout and at a table, a little distance away, Brennan was displaying his wrists of timepieces. 'Hey, Brennan!'

Brennan sent across a gaze of venom, disbelief, moved to them with an exaggerated mime of his infirmities.

'Yes?' he said without deference to Neelan.

'I gave you a nicker to clean the bathroom.'

'You did.'

'But you didn't,' Neelan said.

'A nicker gets you at the bottom of the list,' Brennan pelted him with words. 'For a fiver you can jump the queue.'

'A fiver for a jakes-mopper?'

'It's well you're not important,' Brennan said, on the fringe of profanity. 'You'd kill the effing lot of us.'

Calnan looked down at his drink, smiled behind a mask of boredom.

'Wait!' Mackessy said. 'It'll be done when he has a chance. Right, Brenno?'

Brennan condescended merely to nod.

'It's for the guv'nor's sake,' Mackessy explained it very well. 'We can't expect him to stumble in and out over a slag heap whenever the need arises to use the john or have a hose-down.'

'It'll be done,' Brennan said unconvincingly; he shot a weak dangerous glance at Neelan.

'It could be done hours ago,' Neelan spat at him, 'if you weren't poncing round the market like Marco Polo.'

'Do it!' Calnan said. 'When you get a chance. As soon as possible.'

'Yes,' Brennan said.

Honour seemed to have been satisfied. Brennan moved away, Neelan smiled at the inconsequence of it all.

Saturday, Calnan thought, always had a shrillness about it, a mild euphoria of prisoners at the end of a stretch: Monday morning and bleak abhorrent working hours sat beyond great space of time. It was strange to hate, to suffer, to discard so much of a lifetime. He could look back thirty years and remember his cracked battered hands on the icy steering wheel of a truck, the wind pushing through the pedal slots, chilling his feet, his legs, his knees to the marrow. The empty roads of early morning; Camden Town in frost, huddles of men in doorways, feet stamping, cigarette glows, canopies of vaporised breath about their heads: load on your gang of humanity and aim for Slough or Beckton or Mortlake, wherever the hole was, and the trestles, the lamps. The morning roads were bleak as ghost towns, six o'clock roads before alarms clanged in genteel bedrooms. He remembered the holes and trenches to be hacked and scooped at, until pipes and cables, whole stomachs of them, were exposed. Long days lived with muck. He used to think of young faces behind him, rubber boots awash in a swill of dirt and bilge water, figures crouched under canvas covers, remembering, he supposed, the exaggerated preposterous beauty they had left behind, as they would remember and enhance it decade after decade . . .

Calnan, at the counter, looked at his hands now: big, powerful, unblemished. He had drunk and whored with the best of them but he had kept something, this much, enough to buy him release. He looked around the bar, at the ageing comfort of it, the warmth, even the untidy legacy of Brennan, and felt at ease. It was home.

'Have a drink,' he heard Mackessy saying.

'I have a drink.'

'Top it up.'

'I know how to drink,' he said; and Mackessy, cautious as his smile, knew when to retreat.

Calnan focused Neelan. 'There must be a few pounds in the whip by now?'

'Fair,' Neelan said.

'How much?' Calnan nailed him.

'Rough guess, ton and a half, I'd say.'

'You have the sheets.'

Reluctantly Neelan produced his documentation and Calnan wrote a total on each page. 'Two hundred and fourteen pounds. On paper.' Calnan said.

'You have some very decent men coming into this pub, I can tell you. Not to mention yourself,' Mackessy lauded.

'And of course there's half a dozen names there, with amounts behind them, that haven't paid yet,' Neelan explained. 'People we trust. Like yourself.'

'If they don't pay, bring a straight-edge from the bathroom and put a line through them. You'll have pulled four hundred by tomorrow night.'

'Christ!' Neelan doubted.

'There's an outside chance,' Mackessy conceded. 'A long shot! Unlikely, Cal.'

'Four hundred plus,' Calnan assured them. 'Monday, we'll pin the sheets on the wall there. People have vanity and they like to see their charitable names in public places. A little sop for their generosity.'

Mackessy and Neelan were nodding without much conviction.

'And,' Calnan said, 'you must be congratulated on your store of Christian charity. How do you intend allocating it?' Calnan smiled. 'The money, I mean.'

Such a swingeing query on the heels of a compliment could only be countered by a throwing-back of brandies and smiling calls to Blondie for fresh supplies.

'Try one this time, Cal.'

Blondie looked and read Calnan's refusal and said like a slap, 'The guv'nor passes.' She brought two brandies.

'I was going to have a beer this time,' Neelan said patiently. 'But, as you've jumped the gun, we'll let it go.' They drank and were silent for a little while. 'Barmaids can be too forward at times. You need to take them down a peg or two.'

'What had you in mind?' Calnan asked.

'The Blondie. I'd give her one,' Neelan said with a twist of the lip. 'And then a belt of an ashplant to see her off.'

'The money . . . the money,' Calnan said. 'What have you in mind?'

'Well, of course, flowers . . .' Mackessy said; and indicated some further obvious essentials with a swing of his hand.

'Flowers are expensive,' Neelan said. 'The weather has been against flowers too, unfortunately. And of course there's VAT . . .'

'For four hundred pounds,' Calnan said with all the

hyperbole he could summon, 'you'd leave Kew Gardens a moonscape.' He held them in a stare. 'I thought it might be practical to give him a decent funeral.'

They gaped at Calnan, dumbfounded, incredulous. 'You mean the undertaker?'

'The coffin and all that?'

'That's about it,' Calnan said.

'But he's covered!' Neelan said; he even had to laugh a little to lessen the shock.

'The State's job!' Mackessy explained. 'Over to the State. Duffy was signing on for years. He was a good tradesman except for his hand.'

There was the usual wait. 'Go ahead, go ahead,' Calnan said eventually. 'Tell me about his hand.'

'A simple thing. Throwing scraps to the ducks in Victoria Park. A great nature lover.' Mackessy seemed overcome. 'Pulled something, you see, and it never went back. And of course arthritis set in.'

'Of course,' Calnan said.

'He always carried a diary. Very methodical,' Neelan filled in the picture. 'If you wanted an appointment he always knew when he was free. And, of course, his numbers were in a prominent place.'

'His numbers,' Calnan nodded.

'Insurance and SS. Social Security. In case of accident or worse the ball is in the State's court. Duffy left nothing to chance.'

Calnan never ceased to wonder at the ingenuity of the ergophobiacs: facets of villainy and sainthood were always dazzling and astounding him with each shake of the kaleido-scope.

'So it's a State funeral, is it?' That earned smiles of appreciation.

'You could put it like that, I suppose.' Mackessy's head, as with a nervous disorder, went into little shaking spasms of amusement. Neelan drank and, at once, savoured the excellence of cognac and wit. He raised his glass.

Calnan said, 'So we're left with four hundred pounds?'

'Christ, no!' Neelan said, in shock. 'They'll be flowers, of course, whatever the cost! "From his Old Friends at the Trade Winds." A nice "Gates of Heaven", flowers mounted on a wire frame, you know. Large size, not much change out of a ton for a start. But, on the front of a hearse it looks the thing.'

'Cheap for the Gates of Heaven too, if it gives him the right of way. What about the rest?' Calnan was patient.

Mackessy had been arranging his thoughts in the background and was ready for the rostrum. 'Flowers. A drink for the drivers, the pallbearers, a good drink, not mean. Incidental expenses, here and there. Say, we bid him farewell at the crematorium, all commitments met, and a hundred and fifty to the good. Do you follow me?'

'Of course he follows you,' Neelan said, and held up a hand for silence. 'So, we're back at the Trade Winds. Ten plates of sandwiches at three quid a plate. Brennan's wife is doing the honours. And the balance over the counter to pay tribute to Jim Duffy. Relatives and contributors only. Morgan will keep us up to date on the spending and draw the line at the end of the whip. Then every man for himself. It could hardly be fairer, Cal. The satisfaction of giving will bring happiness to all. Duffy will have been sent off with the proverbial decency of an ancient race. And, of course, yourself! You'll have made a few bob.'

Calnan nodded at the arrogance and arithmetic. Blondie brought him a drink. 'Before we take off for the crematorium,' he said to Mackessy, 'there's one thing: we pin the subscription sheets on the wall.'

'Of course!' Neelan said with the fixed eye of a ferret.

'And a little balance sheet as well.'

'Profit and loss,' Neelan saluted.

'Income and expenditure might be better. Less accurate, of course, but less offensive too.'

At six o'clock Morgan was back to open the doors and

give purpose and direction to the evening. 'I haven't eaten for two days,' Calnan told him. 'I need a lot of food.'

Morgan nodded.

Mackessy and Neelan had moved away in a perusal of foolscap sheets, behind masks of tranquillity. Brennan, wrists exposed, was counselling on the choice and care of chronometers. He had sold two of his exhibits, Calnan noted.

He took a bus to the Angel for his food. There was an old *ristorante* on the unfashionable side, looking across at the arrived gimmicky world of antique and gewgaw. Alfredo, the chef, could nod from his kitchen to Calnan.

Escaloped veal, golden breadcrumbed, cream wine sauce, broccoli, spinach, potatoes sautéed in butter.

Calnan drank a little and let the food smells gather about him.

6

It was hardly more than a short step from Islington to the Trade Winds; three miles, Calnan assessed, as he set out. He liked to walk, it was no effort on such caisson legs to carry his weight. He had eaten Alfredo's food, drunk the house wine, and could still relish the taste, feel the warmth: French wines were powdered and perfumed, hidden away from Calnan's world behind dainty windows, flawed glass, ruched curtains.

The statue of Myddleton, an Islington patriarch of long, long ago, stood on the last triangular scrap of village green with ageing seats and trees yellowed in the late fall, the stumps of countless amputations scattered on their trunks like warts. The breeze was rising again and in a split second of traffic silence a dry rustle wafted down to him. At the public lavatory a drunk, or maybe a deranged old man, shouted something incoherent and was ignored by a zombie stream of urban forbearance. Behind him and the grass patch had been Collins' Music Hall: Calnan had drunk there, watched its last resurgence and sudden decline from entertainment to the sadness of tit, clit and smut. It was an office columbarium now, glass and glaze, part of the great featureless architecture of a strange new world.

Pittas and Greek loaves in shop windows with sides of sheep and seemingly fossilised excretions of sausage-meat somehow reminded him of pot-ovens hanging close down to turf fires and a red ember-bedding on the pot lid to draw and give lightness to soda bread. It assailed him now, and the apron smells of his mother, always vast, always pregnant, he remembered, holding him sometimes against her stomach, making perhaps excuses for inconstant love, such diluted attention. He had been first out, first away, never once back for a death, a marriage, a christening. Nothing. He had disliked the yellow stallion teeth of his father: teeth, a cap, jet-black stubble, leathery hands, he remembered, nothing more. A stranger.

In less than an hour he was back at the Trade Winds and the crush and smoke of Saturday night was being whisked to a froth. Morgan and the lassies moved about, never stopping, never rushing. He nodded, acknowledged salutations with his acceptable mask of distance. Morgan brought him a drink and said, 'Feeling better?'

Calnan nodded.

From somewhere in the depths of the pool Neelan and Mackessy surfaced. Neelan, suddenly, with great ostentation, produced his sub-sheets. 'I thought you'd like to have a scan, Cal. We'll be starting on the evening tour any time now.' He released thumb and index finger to make a snapping competent sound, held the rolled papers like a baton to orchestrate and conduct his business.

Calnan ignored the proffered papers and the perilous implications of audit and surveillance.

'There's your john-henry at the top of the list,' Mackessy said, 'and twenty quid chalked beside it.' He paused to choose a harmonious reverential tone which finally emerged like a broken whisper. 'Every man jack has remarked on your generosity.'

Calnan said obliquely, 'Don't bother to buy drawing pins, I meant to tell you. There's a few upstairs.'

Mackessy groped at what might be humour; Neelan, in shop steward role, was mulling it. 'Drawing pins?'

Calnan nodded away undue importance to so slight a matter. 'For pinning the sheets on the wall,' he said. 'On Monday.'

There was a moment's silence.

'Blue-Tack is the thing now, Cal,' Mackessy said in a spate of helpfulness. 'Very good, very clean. A kind of plasticine compound, I'd say. No holes in the wall or your thumb!'

'Good,' Calnan said; their presence about him now and the exposition of sub-sheets, even to the unobservant, were marks of 'royal' patronage. Neelan ordered drinks: they were still with the brandy.

'No,' Calnan said.

'People are watching,' Mackessy explained. 'They like to see the guv'nor included. A sense of brotherhood at a time of misfortune, you know what I mean?'

'I don't,' Calnan said.

Neelan drummed his fingers on the counter, a figure of worry, unease. 'Were you at the hospital by any chance?' he said suddenly to Calnan.

'I don't like hospitals.'

'I rang the hospital,' Neelan said: and with all the expertise of a chat show dummy awaited the flood of words that silence provokes.

Calnan waited too, drank and looked at him; but it was Mackessy, even in the glare of Neelan, who faltered. 'There's a mystery man somewhere,' he explained.

Neelan made the best of it. 'More than that,' he said. 'We have a crafty bastard on the loose. Personal effects collected and on his way to the undertaker. That's the story.'

'Ah?' Calnan planned a map of confusion for them. 'What's his name?' he said.

'Hospitals are like the nick,' Neelan said. 'No information.'

Calnan agreed. 'You should have called in person.'

'They'd like that!' Neelan stared. Mackessy and he seemed to keep incredulity within reason by dint of enormous effort of will. 'Personal effects are dynamite, you know!' He paused to change key and calm himself. 'I'd say Duffy was carrying at least a ton. He always kept a reserve, you see. He had a secret pocket.'

72

'In his underpants,' Calnan spun it. 'I caught a glimpse of him in the toilet once. A ton at least.'

'Dear Christ!' Mackessy said. 'We tried his pockets before the ambulance came. A few pence was the lot!'

'His underpants!' Neelan said in pale consternation.

Calnan nodded. 'Still, in a public place, it wouldn't do to be seen groping around a dying man's balls.'

Neelan sent a withering scorn at him: as if in such dire circumstances, surgery, even dismemberment, were so far inside the pale as to be commonplace.

'At least a ton, would you say?' Mackessy asked.

'Maybe more,' Calnan said. 'It only takes two fifties to make a ton. Ten notes and you're talking about five hundred flags.'

'Jesus!' Neelan said. Silence contained them for two, three minutes. Calnan stood, pushed away through the crowd, made a charade of telephoning and returned.

'The hospital?' Neelan asked.

Calnan nodded.

'Anything?' Mackessy waited.

'I said I was the Catholic curate at Dalston Junction,' Calnan explained.

Neelan rapped the counter, thought better of back-slapping Calnan, was full of fresh hope. 'Go on!'

'A diary, a broken watch, a tie-clip and one pound thirty-eight and a half pence cash,' Calnan enumerated on his fingers. 'Signed for by "Ronan Mahaffey", his executor.'

'Who? His what?' Mackessy said.

'His executor. There must have been an estate,' Calnan paused convincingly, considering it. 'Property, maybe in Ireland.'

'An estate.' Neelan was almost inaudible, in shock, but he groped back to reality. 'The executor does the winding up,' he explained to Mackessy. 'Arrives at what they call the residue after funeral expenses and all outstanding debts have been met. Does he owe you anything?' he sprung suddenly again at Calnan.

'Not a light.'

Neelan considered the predicament for what seemed a long arduous time of speculation, fought some painful battles with himself. 'Over the years he was in to me for a fair bit,' he said unhappily. 'A fiver here, a tenner there, fifty once, to pay a fine, if my memory serves me. It soon adds up.'

'How much?' Calnan said.

'You could say four hundred.'

'All of that,' Mackessy confirmed at once. 'And going before his Maker, Duffy RIP, would be the last to renege.'

'His clothes?' Neelan suddenly remembered. 'His underpants?'

'The undertaker,' Calnan said. 'His clothes will be his winding-sheet.'

'The undertaker?'

'Canonbury Chapels. The Clincher Casey in Upper Street.' Calnan waited for the shock waves to reach them. 'I rang him just now. Underwear is burned at once, he told me. Suit, collar and tie, a pair of socks, is all Duffy needs for the take-off.' He paused and said, 'No money. Unless it went up in smoke with the rest.'

Neelan said, 'You had the Clincher's number, had you?'

'The hospital had.' Calnan looked at their grief and outrage.

'Up in smoke, my arse!' Mackessy said. 'Into the Clincher's back pocket. That fellow's a wanted man in Cork for twenty years. Going around in schoolgirl's knickers and caught interfering with sheep in some agricultural college. Even goats, some people would tell you.'

'One good thing,' Calnan said, supplying another dimension. 'The funeral is paid for. That'll leave the executor with a few extra quid in the kitty.'

'Hold it! Hold everything! Neelan said; he called for a brandy and said to Calnan, 'For Christ's sake have a drink.' Calnan nodded to Morgan. 'I'm confused, Cal. Addled. A spy

whodunnit on the box wouldn't hold a candle to this balls-up!
What's the executor's address?'

'Private, they said.' Calnan showed sympathy. 'A private
individual, you see. He'll put a notice in Duffy's local paper
eventually, asking to hear from creditors. You can jump in
then. But, of course, you have no proof.'

'Proof?'

'Receipts, IOUs, formalities of that nature.'

'There's such a thing as honour,' Mackessy said. 'A debt of
honour!'

'I suppose there is,' Calnan conceded. 'Tread softly, like a
good man,' he said to Neelan. 'It has been known for the
Law to push these notices in. If Duffy had a bit of form, even
knocking the Social Security for a few quid a week, the
smallest thing, they'd be spreading the net for his mates.'

This produced a great meditative block of silence. Drinks
were gazed at, barely sipped, returned to the counter with a
kind of gentleness as if noise might activate whirring police
wheels and blinding lights of discovery.

Neelan said after a long time, gathering threads again,
'Who's paying for the funeral, then?'

'An American cousin, I'm told. Elmer Devine.'

'An American cousin?' Mackessy clawed for a grip. 'Is
paying the Clincher?'

'Has paid. Cash in advance.'

'The Clincher told you, I suppose?' Neelan was struggling
to arrange the puzzle. 'The Clincher is bad news. Elmer
Devine, he said? He's sure it wasn't Burt Lancaster or
Hopalong Cassidy? There's something wrong, Cal.'

'Your guess is as good as mine,' Calnan said. 'There could
be property in America too.'

Neelan was suddenly overloaded. 'Tomorrow. I'll think
about it tomorrow.' He closed shop. 'I'll sleep on it. With a
clear mind tomorrow I'll strip it down.'

'Elmer Devine?' Mackessy gave it a final toss. 'Devine is an
Irish name. But Elmer?'

Neelan exhaled impatience.

In a little while Calnan said, 'American property. He mightn't even be a cousin, of course.' He carefully dropped a banger in the hot ashes. 'Only time will tell. We'll wait and see.'

Close by now, he could hear Brennan on a gentle *démarche* to his audience, a splendid voyage up the creek of chronology. 'Only two left, gentlemen. And confidentially, the pick of the bunch. The inexperienced man, you see, goes for the flash job. But it's what's behind the face that counts. You look at plain-jane here. Not a second glance. But you're wrong, gentlemen: Swiss, twenty-seven jewel movement, screw-back, watertight, airtight, anti-magnetic, shock-proof . . .'

Out of his poisonous frustration Neelan snapped across him. 'There's a shithouse waiting up there for you, Brennan. Pull your brush out and make a move!'

The words struck: the created sales tension was frittered away in laughter that demeaned Brennan who was more flawed than his watches. He came to the counter, laid a pound before Neelan. 'Clean your own dirt,' he said. 'You little Dublin jack!'

Neelan turned to Calnan. 'Far be it from me to interfere in another man's business. But patrons are patrons. A latchico pushing out duff watches at decent drinking men paying their way, swapping a yarn, gives cause for offence.'

Calnan raised a finger to silence him; he said to Brennan, 'Did you sell Duffy a watch?'

'The week he died, God rest him. A lovely job: luminous dial, lizard skin strap, digital-electronic, up to the minute . . .'

'U/S, the hospital described it,' Calnan said. 'That means, unserviceable.'

Brennan nodded. 'He must have struck it when he collapsed, a considerable impact at that.' He paused. 'A very common occurrence, you can take it from me. At the moment of death, the brain, the whole nervous system is in top gear, you see. The hands shoot out in self-preservation.'

'I see,' Calnan said.

'It was another one of your spuds,' Neelan said. 'It stopped an hour before he died.'

'At the Nag's Head corner,' Mackessy confirmed. 'It put him in a dangerous mood.'

Brennan made an elaborate sign of the cross and seemed to gaze for moments into some other world. 'A premonition,' he said. 'God between us and all harm.'

Mackessy said, 'In the circumstances you should stick a fiver in the whip. Pay respect to the dead.'

'Electricity plays a part too . . .' Brennan eventually emerged from his trance.

'Does it?' Calnan said.

'A buildup of electricity in the body before the final short circuit.'

'A buildup of bollicks!' Neelan said.

'Electricity?' Mackessy was in doubt. 'I read once we're surrounded by electricity.'

Like a conjuror Brennan had a shred of paper on the counter and was rubbing his comb briskly on his lapel. 'The world is a power-house, my dear man,' he said condescendingly to Neelan. When he held the comb close, the scrap of paper jumped to it, as metal to a magnet.

Po-faced, Calnan said, 'Power.'

'By God!' Mackessy said.

'A pity you didn't rub the comb on your nuts,' Neelan said. 'You'd have set fire to the counter. Don't forget you're due a fiver in the whip.'

'Electricity,' Brennan said, unabashed, 'is an invisible force all around us and in every cell of the body. I'm getting back to the watch incident,' he explained to Neelan. 'The power surge of death can stop a watch, you see.'

'Like the electric chair,' Mackessy stated, grappling now more successfully with physics and biochemistry.

'A rough comparison,' Brennan allowed. 'But near enough.'

'A pity it wasn't anti-magnetic,' Calnan said.

Brennan only faltered a moment. 'It was waterproof, of course,' he said. 'But the anti-magnetic job comes a bit dearer.' He unstrapped a model from his wrist and laid it prone on the counter and, as a pointer, used his ball-point pen with the delicacy of a surgeon. 'You have before you the complete model. Screw-on back, anti-magnetic, waterproof...' Mackessy nodded at the addition of each magical quality. 'That little screw-on disc,' he touched it reverently, 'is half your watch.'

Calnan had tired of it. 'What's in it?' he said. 'Uranium?' And Brennan, a second to spare, side-stepped, met the merriment with merriment.

Mackessy said, 'Sharp as a razor, Cal!'

'What will they find at the autopsy?' Brennan was in again, effectively changing pace and mood; grave, undiminished.

'Thrombosis,' Calnan offered. 'Cerebral? Coronary? A very massive occlusion, I suppose.'

'I'd agree with that,' Brennan said.

'Would you?'

'He looked a bit flushed of late. And the veins showing in the eyes. That's another warning light.'

'I didn't know that,' Calnan said.

'I have a full set of *Home Doctor*,' Brennan admitted in part explanation, at least, of such accumulated knowledge. 'Twelve volumes. I picked them up at a Protestant jumble sale.'

'How much?' Neelan asked.

'A fiver. A fiver ten years ago.'

'You wouldn't give a fiver for the *Dead Sea Scrolls* and the *Book of Kells* thrown in for good measure,' Neelan said; he drank morosely.

Mackessy seemed to ponder on twelve volumes of death and disease.

'Thrombosis?' Brennan said loudly, professionally, to Calnan.

'Yes.'

'Cerebral?'

'Could be.'

'I think they have the top of the head off for that.'

'For what?' Neelan blazed with anger; and, behind it, fear.

'The autopsy. A clot on the brain, you see. They must trace it. Trace the fault, so to speak.'

'Like a gas main,' Mackessy said.

'They dig trial-holes for a gas main,' Calnan dropped soberly into the pond.

'Well, if a man is dead, there's no need for exactitude,' Brennan explained. 'Have the lot off. Gives the students a bit of practice for the real thing.'

'And a squint at the brain too,' Mackessy agreed.

Morgan brought Calnan a drink and he pushed them out of his mind and hearing, stared at the neatness of hip and limb of the lassies, the tilt of a chin.

He remembered a blondie in Southend once but now the face had blurred and he had to search behind the darkness of closed eyes for it; and the image shone for only an instant and was gone again. Southend: pearlies in pubs, knees-ups, flat beer, a train ride out on the longest pier splitting the grey water, to a kind of buzzing pile, a fly-infested stool propped above the tide. A day at the seaside. She had smiled at everything, such a tranquil impervious smile, or overpowered him with sudden recitals of facts she had accumulated, journeys she had made, and a whole future of plans bursting at its seams. Men at the pier-end fished without reward on this dolphin of paper cups, the clang and whirr of funland, whirligigs, bandits, what-the-butler-saw. She had smiled at it all, pointed at a speck, a smudge on the horizon: a coaster, seemingly motionless but crawling out to sea. And then suddenly she had moved ahead, flanked by two attentive young men. They were all laughing. He had followed them to the coach, waved to her as they drew away. A patients' outing, the escorts had explained. She had seemed so much part of a summer's day; but visiting her, an alien, at the end of endless passages and closed doors, visiting a giggling characterless face, a torrent of language that meant nothing and the silences as she listened to someone else, her madness had smitten him like the full swing of a sledge-hammer. He hoped she was dead a long time ago. She had been a little cockney blondie, leggy and smart as Morgan's number one.

Bar noises impinged on him again, giving him feeling and shape. A very evil-looking young man with a part-shaven tinted head studied Brennan who peered into the bowels of a watch with a black professional eyepiece. Neelan and Mackessy seemed hopeful of bloodshed.

'Well?' the Mohican said.

Brennan focused with great precision. 'Ah!' he said, 'I have it! A shaft. A secondary shaft down behind the flywheel. A million to one chance but that's life.'

'Not the crankshaft, I hope,' Neelan said, 'or maybe if you take another squint through your goggle, it might be the hydraulic system.'

Calnan sat and pondered with the detachment of an ageing radio listener, hearing old jokes worth a thought but not a smile. Brennan, making a few pence per watch, was a re-charged entrepreneur, tireless in sales battles; with a brush in hand, he was shifty as a skiv. And Mackessy and Neelan too, created their own false importance, guarded it like terriers.

In godfather mood Brennan said, 'I'll make you an offer you can't refuse.' He pushed across the display model of a few moments before. 'Yours,' he said to the Mohican. He nodded regretfully as he coffined the rejected piece in a matchbox and stowed it away. 'Yours,' he repeated and sang out once more the litany of its magic. 'For just a quid! This thing in my pocket was a dud, a banger, and bangers last a mile or maybe forever. You have there a thoroughbred, a Roller.' He paused and said quietly, 'For just another quid, that's all! Couldn't be fairer.'

'If I have to come back with this Roller,' the Mohican said, loose-lipped, tonelessly, 'you're in bother, grandad.'

Brennan laughed at the outlandishness. 'There's years of wear in that piece of jewellery,' he said.

'And I never pay out quids in a swapshop!'

'My dear man,' Calnan said eventually with just a glimmer of sympathy, 'whenever it's important for you to know the time it might be cheaper to take a taxi down to Big Ben. And if there's going to be bother this week or next, have it out on the street or at the traffic-lights or at the pub up the road. Not here.'

'Who's this crock of dogshit?' the young man asked Brennan.

Silence wrapped them like a plastic vacuum-skin. Even Neelan blanched at the outrage. Mackessy pushed out each word with immense effort. 'The guv'nor. Mr Calnan, the guv'nor,' he said.

The shaven head, the hard stony face said to Calnan, 'Button your fat lip, Fido, or they'll be pushing you round in a handcart like a pile of melted corpse-grease.'

Calnan drank: he might not have heard him.

'And if you want a pound,' he told Brennan, 'come and get it.' He pushed his way through the crowd to some table out of sight.

Morgan's disinterested eyes missed nothing; he saw the unmistakable negative in Calnan's face and let sleeping dogs lie.

The placidity of Calnan extended to them all: it was nothing, hardly a ripple on the pond. A kind of jollity returned.

'I'll bet that fellow never misses a football match,' Mackessy said with a flash of sour humour.

'Boots and bicycle chains polished up for Saturday night,' Neelan said, 'and a can of glue in the back-pocket.'

Mackessy, a little cast down at such a peaceful dénouement, hardened. 'They have the whole continent of Europe terrorised. The Brits, the yobbos. Not to mention places nearer home and the heart's desire.'

'Leave politics to the politicians,' Neelan said *ex cathedra*; and Mackessy was repentant.

Brennan stood in isolation, still trembling a little from an encounter he felt he had handled with commendable expertise. Now he needed some conversational thunderbolt to centralise himself again. 'That was bad about the bomb,' he said with his usual studied vagueness.

'Bomb?' Mackessy said.

'And fortunate too, of course.'

Neelan gazed at him unyieldingly, a veteran defender, weary of tactics. Calnan seemed deep in some reverie.

Mackessy twitched in the vacuum. 'Fortunate?' he said, at the end of patience.

'A bomb in the British Museum,' Brennan said. 'Under some priceless Chinese collection too.' Brennan was in command, summarising with the ease of a commentator. 'I caught it on the six o'clock news,' he said.

Mackessy grew aware of his role. 'Much damage?' he asked.

'None.'

'Ah?'

'It didn't go off,' Brennan said. 'Faulty mechanism.'

Calnan finished his drink. 'It must have been one of your arsehole watches,' he said. 'Get that bathroom cleaned up. That'll take you ten minutes. And be down here half an hour before the bell clangs. The first bell.'

Brennan slid away.

Neelan said, 'I don't know how you stick it, Cal.'

'That kind of jack-the-lad act with watches,' Mackessy shook his head. 'A one-way ticket for the bust-up.'

'You handled it well,' Neelan said.

Mackessy agreed and called a drink. 'A bad package, that young fellow. Imagine talking like that to a man nearly three times his age.'

Calnan sat silent, hardly listening; he could sense bother, almost smell it; and he thought a little wearily of how he might handle it or let it ride.

'Weekend drinkers,' Neelan said with the dismissive pooh-

pooh of an expert.

'A National Front yobbo,' Mackessy spat. 'They have the Pakis down in Shoreditch under siege.'

'His name is Murphy,' Calnan said. 'He has a mother and a father walking up there to Mass every Sunday morning. I remember when they each had a hand and he was trotting between them.'

Eventually Mackessy said, 'It's a funny world.'

'Put blame where it belongs,' Neelan decreed. 'Brennan is a bollicks.' It was safer ground, he felt. 'What would you do?' he put it to Mackessy. 'What would you do if a chancer sold you a pig in a bag?'

'I'd have his guts for garters!'

'Well, there you are.'

Mackessy was pleased with the role of avenging angel: he thought about it and summed up. 'That young man has red blood in his veins. He won't be messed about. That's it in a nutshell.'

He and Neelan drank and felt unease at the silence and stillness of Calnan. 'Well, it's time to do a round for Duffy,' Neelan said, requisitioning the begging-box and the clipboard. 'A good crowd tonight. You must strike in the last half-hour when it's steam up and holes open.' Drinks downed, they were ready for action. And then, as if on behalf of the world of beleaguered gentlefolk, Mackessy said, 'Brennan! A shame decent people have to deal with con-men and thimbleriggers.'

'The bathroom,' Calnan said. 'That was a nice gesture with your mother's ring. Generous.' He was still as a ventriloquist. They moved away. Neelan's face was red with unspent bitterness.

Time was speeding on towards the end of Saturday salvation and Calnan assessed each passing moment. After twenty minutes he said to Morgan, 'We have bother. Send the lassies to the toilet for five minutes. And stay inside the counter.'

Morgan paused, considered it, nodded.

Calnan knew the rumble of pub ructions, a cocktail of sound: then shattering glass, a rattattoo of feet, the male and female bellow and whinny, a strange gathering bombilation of panic. Brennan, brush in hand, in a high speed hobble, went past, eyes crying in fear, his face painted in sweat.

'Sit on the stairs and lock the door,' Calnan told him.

The epicentre of the storm was by the furthest door: a table upturned, the legs torn off and wielded to smash mirrors and glassware, whatever was ornate and fragile; beer from skittering exploding glasses frothing in the air; a stool pitched across the counter to crash against the cabinet and bring down a glittering rain of debris.

Just two of them, Calnan noted; they were almost spent with flailing and weaving now, ready to leave. Sixty seconds is a long time in a pub-smash. Calnan went through the door nearest to him, moved to where they would make their exit and waited. With his open palm, broad as a spade, and the whole weight of his body behind the swing, he met the surprised face of Brennan's dissatisfied customer, catapulted him against the door; his comrade in destruction was trapped in the porch, hands held up in surrender.

Calnan pointed down at the red wealed face, a bleeding mouth and nose, his eyes struggling back to focus. 'Pick him up,' he said. 'Take him where he belongs. And I know I won't see you again.'

He watched their car out of sight and walked in across the desolation, the crunch of glass, costing each scar and blemish, burning with anger.

In half an hour the towels were up; the last stragglers eased out to the pavements where they stood trapped in little webs of conversation, reluctant to escape. Morgan locked the doors, his staff washed the last of the glasses, left them in wire trays to dry; he poured drinks for them, left only the pilot light at the till burning, drank a tot of rum himself.

'Sleep tight, guv'nor,' Morgan said; Calnan almost smiled. The blondie looked at him with moist kindly eyes, admiring such a great ugly bulk. 'Goodnight, guv'nor,' she said in a soft affectionate voice. The door snapped shut behind them.

Calnan watched, listened. Brennan and Mackessy swept up the battlefield of glass and rubble; Neelan brought a plastic bin, a shovel, from the cellar. In the dim light a kind of peace and normalcy returned. Strange bedfellows, Calnan thought, watching them in the shadows.

He poured pints of beer for them. 'Look,' Brennan said. 'my hands are trembling.'

'I'll be in bed in five minutes,' Calnan announced. 'Finish your drinks.'

'We could use a half an hour,' Neelan said. 'Clearing glass is a dirty job. Depressing.'

'I know that.'

'Just a couple of rounds,' Mackessy smiled. 'Friends don't take advantage.'

Brennan said, 'I could use a drink, myself, Cal.' His fingers were pinching at his coat and trouser legs. 'Pub battles are very upsetting.'

Calnan looked stonily at them, pondered, examined his watch, studied them again. It was a quarter to midnight.

'A half an hour,' he said. 'After that if you want drink, buy a bottle, take it with you.'

Behind him, Neelan smiled his contempt. They waited for Brennan, indebted by their labours, to buy. 'He wants three brandies,' Neelan said.

When Calnan brought the drinks they were men of sub stance, the gas fire bathing them in fixity of tenure. 'Don' get too comfortable,' he advised them. 'You'll need rest There's a bathroom waiting for the craftsmen up there.' And to Brennan: 'Be here on the dot tomorrow with a wire brush And if I see your eye on a watch or a clock, you're dead Remember that.'

Neelan said suddenly, 'We had a bit of bad luck with th whip tonight.'

'The bust-up. We were caught in the bust-up,' Mackess

85

said. 'It could have been a diversion of course. Dips work like that,' he explained. 'It was going to be a record night too.'

'You were dipped?'

'The box was dipped,' Neelan said.

'How much?'

'Over the ton, I'd say.'

'At least. Another twenty maybe,' Mackessy confirmed. 'A funeral whip too. Would you believe it! Bastards like that don't deserve a day's luck!'

Calnan looked hard at them. 'No luck at all,' he said; he went behind the bar and poured himself a drink.

7

*D*IPPED. Calnan stood shielded by the display cabinet, filled a measure of brandy, drank it and filled his glass again. Anger was never a raging ongoing passion in Calnan's mind, only a mild abrasive thread of thought that found its own insulation with time; or had suddenly to be plucked out, roots and all.

He came outside the counter, ignored the silent trio in the aura of the gas fire and went to the scene of battle. Glass-dust shone in even the faint glimmer of street light; dark ugly blots of spilt beer pocked the carpet, lay pooled in the lino strip by the counter; an upturned table with two legs was pushed against the wall, its sundered members discarded like gangrenous limbs in the rubbish bin. Calnan remembered where he had bought it, how much he had paid: details of effort and expense remained always in his mind. A world of planned obsolescence shocked him a little; he could examine spent ball-point pens, razors, cigar tubes, empty spirit bottles, conscious of a skill that had shaped them and some final price to be paid for destruction. A large pale rectangle on the facing wall had housed a bevelled mirror, thick as Edwardian pride; chunks of it had exploded to the corners and into the shadows of seats; the hanging canopy of glasses above the counter had been sabred to a few ragged stems; and on a shelf of the wounded display cabinet advocaat dripped from a shattered bottle like the death of some obscene ritual. The insurance would pay, Calnan thought, and then thrash him with nine-tailed premiums. He thought of the yobbos and corpse grease, a turnip head, a greasy sergeant, the gold Roman numerals of the church clock.

There was work to be done now. From the gas fire uneven desultory overtures were gapped by silences; drinks worked in peaks and troughs; soon they would be in full spate. Dipped. Calnan smiled humourlessly, strode the length of the bar in silence and climbed the stairs to his room.

He heard Neelan say, 'Brandy at the bar and brandy at the bedside. You could put an air to that.'

Brennan was laughing; and then he said, 'That was a fine piece about Duffy. The poetry. Death waiting in the wings.'

'To take him back to God. Beautiful,' Mackessy said.

'It should have been read in a whisper,' Neelan said. 'That fat man grunts like an animal. He made a bollicks of it.'

'I thought that,' Brennan said. 'But he couldn't destroy the words. They'll last for ever.'

'Well said!' Mackessy added and silence fell again.

The bathroom was still deep in rubble, Calnan noted as he passed. In his room he sat on the bedside, telephoned Cassie and very carefully laid his plans with her. It took a little while and he smiled once or twice. Then he worked at the accumulated notes from under his pillow, and from the safe, and with unexpected neatness and method smoothed and arranged them; he seemed to care inordinately for each piece of paper. Money, he respected; once in its absence, now in plenty. From his breast-pocket he took rubber bands, made tidy bundles, entered them meticulously on a lodgement slip and reached his total.

A great deal of money, he thought: two, three decades ago the price of a man's house, a door number, a garden patch. Now a weekend's beer money. He had two leather night-safe bags beneath his bed: the notes and slip had to be pushed and forced into the inadequate space. He snapped the locks on them and hid them in the bedclothes. When he reached the bar again the faces were warm and smiling. Mackessy tendered a fiver. 'Would you do the honours again, Cal? And include your good self.'

Calnan looked at the clock and nodded. 'I have a drink,' he said quietly.

'You made a great job of the poem. Didn't he?' Mackessy said to Neelan.

'First class.'

'The wife was remarking recently,' Brennan began, 'how you can recognise every great star from the voice . . . Cagney . . . Bogart, Jimmy Durante, Peter Lorre . . .'

'Sidney Greenstreet,' Neelan said.

'You have a great voice, Cal.' Mackessy smiled his appreciation. 'A great gift.'

'Unforgettable,' Neelan said.

It was a space after twelve when Cassie rapped lightly on the window, held her face close to the figured glass, silenced them.

'It's that little one from across the road!' Neelan said.

'Ah, the nurse!' Mackessy brightened. 'Neat as ninepence.'

'Physiotherapist,' Brennan corrected him. 'And private patients only, mark you.' He lowered his voice. 'The bedridden and that kind of thing. A vocation really.'

Neelan snickered. 'They all do a turn on the side. When the money is down the legs are up. I'd say she's bedridden all right!' Neelan was still relishing the thought when Calnan ushered her in.

The gas fire gilded her from head to toe. She was small, striking, almost beautiful, seeming to hide her curves and gracefulness and inadvertently expose them in a thoughtless moment. She was apologising to Calnan for the lateness of the hour. Calnan introduced them and kept Neelan until last. 'All friends of the deceased,' he was saying. 'But this is the headman. A lot of work put in, forty-eight hours of it for the final tribute.'

Cassie smiled at him; and a kind of infantile bashfulness brought a show of teeth and downcast eyes to mask Neelan's face in gommery.

'So you're the marvellous selfless man collecting for Jim!'
she said. 'Jim Duffy. Dear Jim. He was an occasional patient.'
She held out a tenner to Neelan. 'A small donation. I thought
I'd catch Cal before bedtime. I had no idea I'd meet you, Mr
Neelan. Jim Duffy always spoke so well of you. News of his
death shocked me.'

Mackessy piously crossed himself.

'Mr Mackessy, there . . .' Neelan waved perfunctorily in
his direction, '. . . gave me a hand of course,' he conceded.

Cassie merely nodded and shone her smiling face on Neelan
again; and he was stricken. 'A drink!' He clicked his fingers
towards Calnan. 'A drink, guv'nor!'

'Orange juice,' Cassie said. 'I'll only stay a minute or two.'
She sat on a stool, close to Neelan, facing him, golden legs
crossed, her admiration reaching out to him. He took from
her gently the ten-pound note with thumb and index finger,
the other digits taking off like Scottie's ducks.

'No name,' she said. 'Just anonymous. I'd prefer that.'

'A fine gesture!' Brennan had got to his feet. 'A saintly
gesture. My name is Brennan.'

'The best pub-cleaner in east London,' Neelan demolished
him with praise. 'Toilets, cellar-drains, everything. Put a mop
in his hand and you have a genius.'

Cassie said to Brennan, 'It's good to have friends.'

She sipped her orange juice, glancing from one to another.
Behind their fawning masks they were scurrying in confusion,
chasing the scripty phrases to win her attention, her approval.

'Physiotherapy is a big field,' Brennan said.

'He was found in a big one,' Mackessy winked, sparked off
an avalanche of unwarranted amusement; Brennan made the
best of it; Cassie shared her laughter with Neelan.

At the counter, hardly in the range of the gas fire, Calnan,
on a stool, was a shadowy bulk. He was thinking of Duffy,
not with compassion but with a faint bias of pity and anger.
So many Duffys, so many years, so many whips. In the early
navvy days there had been a watchman on a site by Waterloo

Station: a big man once, dying then; each night, pushed
against the red coke of the fire-devil, a countdown for his
flight to Leytonstone Cemetery. People remembered his
savage strength, measured it in the length of cuttings and
cubic yards of muck per day he could leave behind him; the
feeds of drink he had endured, the whores greedy for his
custom. Calnan had gone to Leytonstone for the burial. He
had never seen a common grave: the big skeleton in his
coffin laid on other coffins, the grave left gaping for the
next, and the next. It was a remote untended corner of the
cemetery. Calnan had been the only mourner and when the
cleric – who might have been Calvin, Catholic or Latter
Day Saint – had set off on his long scabrous trudge back
to gravel paths and his mortuary chapel there had been an
awful sense of desolation and loss. An electric train had
clattered along the embankment beside him: a long fading
rattle of warning.

Calnan looked around the ageing security of his bar with
affection. He drank a little. Conversation at the fire, steady
and competitive now, reached him again.

'So Duffy was a patient?' Brennan sounded Cassie out,
hiding his curiosity.

'None of our business,' Neelan rapped him.

'Quite right,' Mackessy confirmed. 'Professional ethics.'

'Confidentiality, if that means anything to the Home
Doctor,' Neelan said.

Cassie, with great tenderness, smoothed the ruffled Neelan,
thanked him with a sudden little pout of her lips. 'Oh, it was
only a little thing. His arm gave him trouble from time to
time.'

Calnan smiled.

'A tragedy,' Mackessy said, 'when an artist is maimed.'

'I could give him relief,' Cassie said. 'A cure was unreachable.'

Neelan raised his glass. 'He suffered in silence.'

The heroic figure of Duffy duck-feeding in Victoria Park,

smitten by some envious god, brought a warm glow of silent amusement to Calnan.

Brennan was hardly convinced. 'Victoria Park, wasn't it?' He expertly baited the hook and cast.

Cassie nodded. 'Saving a drowning child.'

In the explosive silence Calnan said, 'He was a fine swimmer, God rest him.'

On such treacherous ground now Mackessy's tactics were exemplary: an instant change of pace and style. 'Did you know he was a very religious man?' he asked Cassie.

'I could believe it,' she said.

'He came from a bleak part of the old country, the Atlantic side, rocks and stones but close to the mysteries of life. Year after year he meant to go back with his hand, hoping the last hope for the only cure. There was an apparition, you see.'

'A divine visitation, you could call it,' Neelan explained it for Cassie and looked to Calnan for his imprimatur.

'UFOs,' Calnan said.

Calnan could remember from early schooldays what still seemed the horrendous profanation of a contrived place of wonder-working: the news put abroad of some strange epiphany of blood and miracle; and the pilgrims, whole or infirm, choking the roads to a cabin ringed by hooks and hawkers with a whole range of 'sacred' talismans, even precious water in iodine bottles small as candle stumps or matchboxes. He could remember the frightening chorus of public prayer sent heavenwards and a growing display of crutches left behind by the shriven. It had been a hoax, of course, and the perpetrators had fled with their spoils to foreign parts. And to awful unnatural death too, it was said. Calnan used to wonder about the crutches. Did all the suddenly disabused unfortunates cry out, fall down and die, he had often pondered.

'UFOs?' Neelan said with carefully judged mild reproof. 'There's many would disagree with you.'

'I didn't think Duffy was a religious man,' Brennan said.

'Well, you hardly knew him except to sweep round him or empty his ashtray,' Mackessy dismissed him.

'Religion is a private thing,' Neelan said tonelessly. 'Something to be talked about with his friends. Private.'

'Yes,' Cassie said.

'Did he ever mention America?' Neelan asked with an unexpectedness and ease that left Mackessy gaping.

'Oh yes,' Cassie said. 'There was an American connection, I think.'

Mackessy said, almost exceeding the speed limit, 'Duffy. He wasn't short a bob or two.'

There was silence.

'He used to talk about Elmer Devine,' Neelan probed. 'Boston or Philadelphia, I'm not sure.'

'I think I might have heard that name,' Cassie said; and she remembered, 'He paid me in dollars occasionally.'

'Duffy? Dollars?'

'I used to warn him about carrying so much money,' she said.

'Oh, he always held a couple o' ton. Friends knew that.' Neelan's hands were restless in excitement.

'That's not a lot really,' Cassie said. 'It was much more than that. Foolhardy, I told him. Walking about with hundreds of pounds. In times like these.'

There was a sudden vacuum; only the breath of the gas fire, the occasional stretch of metal. Calnan smiled in the shadows. With ease Cassie moved through the plot, improved it.

'Now, I must go,' she said; she raised her orange juice to them and drank. 'Early appointments tomorrow. Today! Morning only. Sunday afternoon and evening is my day of rest. A piece of a day at any rate.' She smiled to them all. 'You're his good friend,' she said to Neelan and kissed him on the cheek. She whispered something close to his ear.

Calnan stood ready to see her out; he drained his brandy. 'After the cremation,' he said, 'we're having a little funeral gathering. I know these friends here would welcome you. A great amount of money donated, you see.'

Neelan sent out a groan of apology for his oversight; Mackessy held his hands high in penitence. Brennan said, 'Money! A spontaneous gesture from his friends. A flood of generosity. Embarrassing, almost.'

'Flowers, general expenses, a worthy send-off, a couple of hours of food and drink for his butties to sit in remembrance.' Neelan paused. 'We lost over a ton, over a hundred pounds, that is, tonight.'

'The kitty was dipped, turned over, money stolen,' Mackessy explained it in anger and grief. 'A bit of unpleasantness. Skinheads, yobbos on the war-path. The bar down there is a shambles.'

Neelan said reassuringly, 'There's a quid or two left in the kitty still. We'll stretch it as best we can. It'll be no mean do.' He stood apart, the scarred unvanquished warrior. 'Even if we must dig deep ourselves or go on the slate. Cal, a guv'nor of the old school, knows our form, never lets the side down.'

'My God!' Cassie said in a great simulation of shock and distress. 'A funeral collection! Could people stoop so low? Are there really people like that on our streets?' She looked at Calnan.

'We'll manage somehow,' Calnan said.

'You weren't injured?' she said unhappily to Neelan.

Mackessy said, 'I had a couple of ribs near enough pushed in.'

'Oh, a few jabs here and there.' Neelan smiled bleakly at its unimportance.

'My dear boy!' she said and Neelan trembled.

Calnan guided her to the door.

Mackessy suddenly called out, 'Did you ever meet his friend, Mahaffey?'

She turned. 'Mahaffey? No,' she said. 'A strange name too. I rarely forget a name. Or a face.' She smiled to Neelan.

As she waved back from the pavement Mackessy was loud

94

in soliloquy. 'These ribs will be a sight tomorrow, black and yellow and sore as a scald . . .'

Calnan returned. 'Finish your drinks,' he said. 'I need sleep. We can see Duffy tomorrow. Before they screw the lid down.'

'At the Clincher's?' Neelan asked.

'The Canonbury Chapels of Rest,' Calnan told him. 'Five o'clock. That's a concession.'

'It might be interesting to talk to the Clincher.'

'It could be,' Mackessy said.

They drank slowly, lingering, glancing out at the night, thoughtful crafty men, wary, unsure of themselves, of each other. Calnan watched the tightness of Brennan's mouth, a sullenness in his eyes. His ruthless dismissal from importance by Neelan and Mackessy had stung like acid and still burned.

'She seems a nice little thing,' he said to Neelan. 'Of course people talk.'

'About what?' Neelan's chin jutted for the strike.

'Well, people always talk, don't they?'

'About what, Brennan?'

'She could be a high-class brasser, maybe. A home help for the bedridden, like you said.'

Neelan, on the hook, clamped his teeth.

'Duffy must have spent a few pounds there. Or a few bucks, I suppose.' Brennan stood up in calm triumph. 'Middle-aged virgin billy-goats!' He shook his head. '. . . Get the taste in their mouths and run ravenous.'

Neelan slid into martial poise. 'Duffy is dead, Flip-flop!'

'Finish your drinks,' Calnan doused it. He turned off the gas fire and the bleak pilot light from the till found ugliness everywhere. He stood over them.

'You're definitely closed, Cal?' Mackessy asked. 'With all the talk tonight the drink was neglected.'

Calnan's lazy glance at him was enough.

'We'll take a half bottle of brandy with us.' Neelan dropped a twenty on the wet table so that Calnan had to reach for it.

Brennan aligned himself. 'The guv'nor's the gaffer. I'm for the road.'

'Together ... together,' Calnan clustered them. Neelan drank from the brandy bottle as they were herded out.

It was one-thirty, Sunday morning; the juggernauts were slumbering; cars, even distant ones, were audible rushing in and out of earshot. Unease like a shifty emptiness was in Calnan's gut. It was one of those nights, he thought. Or mornings.

He put on a heavy lined Burberry, fitted night safe bags and brandy in voluminous pockets and went out into the sharp grip of November. The Chinese takeaway lit the pavements, was empty of customers. Wang, the hired proprietor, was in the doorway: small, aproned, emaciated, cheek-bones jutting, his smile a grimace of closed eyes, a mouthful of teeth. Calnan called him Wang because it was Wang's Oriental Food. To Wang Calnan was Mister Trade Winds: he had all the singsong lisps and foibles of third-rate television comics. Inside the tiny shop, beyond the counter and yellow hanging strings of beads, were shrunken miniature people: three dwarf children, a mother, a grandparent. An infant crawled about like an ageing house-pet. They would close at four o'clock.

'Lock up, Wang,' Calnan told him. 'Only cops and robbers at this hour.'

Except for his lisping 'Mister Trade Winds' he never spoke. Teeth and gums and a hissing deference were his response.

'I hope the bastards pay you well.' Calnan strode down the empty street.

Cypriot-Greeks and Turks, Pakistanis, Indians, Blacks of Africa and West Indies had seized the crumbling Victorian shops and made ugly hawking-posts of them. The Durex Shop was the only Cockney, and he was of Polack blood, born in Wapping; a cantankerous little pear-shaped wasp who at polling times sported 'Vote Conservative' like an up-market aphrodisiac. A general erection, Calnan thought, looking over at his window and a dreary dump of surgical impedimenta. A tarpaulin on the corner news-stand flapped.

Calnan scanned the pavements, the immediate ground, and with his key opened the night safe chute at the bank: he heard his money-bags slide and the thud as they hit the bottom. He drank a little from his bottle. Passing the police station, a rozzer on the steps said, 'How's life, Cal?'

'Exciting,' Calnan told him without stopping. 'I was arrested on Friday for pissing on graves. Irish piss.'

'I heard,' the rozzer called after him, full of laughter. 'Guilty of course!'

'Of course,' Calnan said.

He walked the long stretch from Dalston to Shoreditch Church and stood looking at the roads fanning out to Hackney, Bethnal Green, Gardiner's Corner, the City, London Bridge, Clerkenwell. This was his London, always traces of elegance but like himself growing old. Shoreditch Church, at the gates of the City, was always reassuring in the stillness of early morning.

He walked a little further into Spitalfields. The market would soon be stirring. In the back-doubles, dossers, drop-outs, long-distance men, tramps, slept on the cardboard wrappings and discards of the market; empty wine bottles, beer cans, dotted this bed of wild flowers and there was urine and excrement in the shadows. A young Scottish face, un-shaven for months – long nails, terrible eyes – threatened him with mutilation, death. An ageing whore exposed everything, made an obscene shunt of her hips and fell in her drunkenness. Her profanity followed him to the end of the alley-way and beyond.

He surfaced again at Bishopsgate, by Liverpool Street Station, and moved on towards Moorgate and City Road and on to the Angel at Islington where he caught a night bus to Dalston. It was crammed tight with postal workers from the acres of sorting-space and the white glare of Mount Pleasant: fourteen hours clocked up, they smoked or drowsed.

Hardly anyone talked. Sunday would be blessed sleep in darkened bedrooms.

It had turned four-thirty when he let himself into the Trade Winds again. His body was warm from the hours of walking, his feet were a little tired. There would be no sleep, he knew. It was another day.

He climbed the stairs to the floor above his bedroom. There was an escape-ladder with a hinged balanced trapdoor to the flat roof. He stood out on the asphalt surface, between two towering corbelled chimneys with moulded pots dainty as vases. He couldn't remember when he had stood there last. Ten years, perhaps longer. He had meant to watch the royal motorcade from there in the Jubilee year but the monarch and her prince had come and gone before the bar could empty, with such indecent haste that they might have left a cake in the oven or a light burning in the toilet.

He drank long and comfortingly from his bottle: it gave life and would be death, he knew. He hoped the end would be a thunder-flash, no more.

He could see, in the near distance, the roof and stark iron cross of the church where he had never attended, even for corpse arrivals or funeral Masses. Survival had prised him away from conformity; and God seemed neither more distant nor reachable. Years ago the parish priest had called, a spare balding man, past middle age. Even his hands were austere; a bleak smile was a flood of warmth. He was a Cornishman, he told Calnan. His fingers were ice-cold. They sat in the empty bar on a darkening late February afternoon when hope is at a premium for the loners and the sapless. Calnan had brought pale sherry.

'You don't come to see us very often.'

'Never,' Calnan said.

'The Landlord of the Inn is observed, you know. His house is a landmark. A respected man. People follow.'

'That was a long time ago,' Calnan said.

He nodded slowly; his eyes were moist with illness or

emotion. He sipped the sherry from silence to silence. 'Everything is changed,' he said eventually.

Calnan nodded.

'The Mass was beautiful once,' he said. 'Yellow candle-flame, altar linen, curtained tabernacle doors, the bread held aloft, the sanctuary bell, the hush behind me of people in the shadows of a church.' His voice had hardly been a whisper but breathing was short and tight. 'It was a half an hour of peace with ourselves.'

'Yes,' Calnan said.

'Now it's a round of standing and sitting, a time of shuffling. I'm a performer.'

'Yes,' Calnan said.

'A pastry-cook. A television pastry-cook.'

Calnan had seen him to the door and thanked him for coming. There had been the bleak smile then like a sunburst and a little movement of his hands. He had lasted a few months more and been taken away to some place of convalescence. Calnan had liked him.

He leant now against the parapet of the roof. Light, like the pale fringe of a tide, was barely showing in the east and a universe of chimney-pots, gables, spires, tower blocks, even a single tree, were black as ink against it.

Sunday. Calnan drank. He went down to the littered bathroom to shave; and to his red bedroom where he changed: underwear, a fresh shirt, tie, socks, a sober deep grey suit that he liked. He blacked and polished his shoes. When the doorbell rang it was Brennan. Seven o'clock!

'I haven't got a wire brush, Cal,' Brennan said. 'I'm sorry.'

'Just clean the place properly,' Calnan said quietly.

'I came early.'

'I can see that.'

Calnan looked at the morning light on the remnants of glass and litter. He could feel angry at the loss of possessions. Morgan would open at twelve. Sunday midday drinking had a trace of dignity, with shirts and ties and perhaps even a rarely seen spouse . . .

At five he would move towards Upper Street to the Clincher's courtesy and reverence and a last glimpse of Duffy in repose.

The carillon in the church tower struck up a hymn at nine o'clock. Calnan went down to Ari the Greek's caff on the High Road.

Ari brought him the paper. 'Big one, Cal?' he asked.

'Very big,' Calnan said.

8

Good food brought a special kind of peace that lasted a long time; even when its taste had gone reluctantly the memory loitered. There might be finer things than tenderloin beef, wild mushrooms bruised on top, black underneath, dripping their juices, and hot Greek soda bread, Calnan thought. There just might be. He looked across at the huge obtruding mural facing him: sea, sand, sky, a cubist hillside village, burning sun and a mountain rising up to snow: everything spoiled by a mad enthusiasm to colour, magnify, flatter.

Ari emerged from the back, letting a phrase or two of bouzouki music escape to the dining-room where Calnan sat alone. Soon it would be a den of old men, playing at cards, drinking thick syrupy coffee, adding hot water to the murky lees, puffing out cigarette smoke which seemed powerless against their ageless vitality. Later, the heavy gang, the gambling men would converge – entrepreneurs, crooks, the hooked – to be given the deference of secrecy and comfort in the back lounge, a forbidden city. Ari would arrange for them drink and food; and women to ease the fevers of bankroll battles. And take his cut of course. Ari drove a Merc and was punctilious in matters domestic: his wife, a well-groomed caparisoned mare, proclaimed his generosity to the world; the education of children obsessed him. It hadn't struck him that education might find more comfort in verse or theatricals than in the smoky home-from-home fleshpots of Kingsland.

Over-education was a dangerous thing, Calnan thought. Even on hallowed playing-fields or under dreaming spires a great care was taken to leave space for ruthlessness.

A sizeable detached in Palmers Green housed Ari's brood; school fees were paid and Ari's wife, hennaed in her suburban world, could drive to coffee and gossip or submit to grey days of motionless ennui. It was a long way to Dalston where Ari liked, from time to time, to talk and joke with nice young truant boys and give them little presents.

'How was it, Cal?' he asked.

Calnan nodded.

'Nice meat. Fourteen ounces for you. The best. I think you like the mushrooms too? Special.'

'Fine,' Calnan said.

'Good for the jump, Cal!'

'I stay on the flat now.'

Ari laughed, sobered, looked out at the quiet of Sunday morning. He returned to Calnan and said, 'Plenty stuff downstairs now.'

'Twelve cases,' Calnan said.

'Vodka, gin, Scotch, cognac? All threes, Cal?'

Calnan waited. Ari seemed to pull a price out of the air. Calnan paid him in twenties and fifties.

'Tomorrow OK, Cal? Today?'

'Ring Morgan,' Calnan said. 'He'll know. Tell him I have a lot of problems.'

Ari poured measures of Metaxa and they drank. 'A good man, Morgan,' he said. 'Very honest.'

'You tried him?'

Ari smiled. 'I try everybody.'

Calnan suddenly laughed and thought that unpleasantness might possibly recede as the day grew up. He said, 'Everyone pinches in the liquor game. Honest ones know when to stop.'

Ari was a fence for booze, fags, a joint, a sniff, precious metals, frozen food, even potato crisps. Cash down, small profit, turnover quick as a flip. A lot of irons, a lot of fires.

Calnan was looking at the vast garish mural of Mediterranean homeland.

'My son,' Ari said. 'Fifteen only. He tried too hard, you think?'

'A bit,' Calnan said. 'You have a place there?'

'Big bastard Turk has it now. Money too. Money, house, land.' He smiled at Calnan. 'They can keep my rocks and stones, Cal. Bank balance? Like this,' he measured half an inch with thumb and forefinger and laughed. 'Here I make money every day. You make money every day.'

'A little.'

Ari's great surge of flinty merriment could have been real. He said, 'When I go for liquor licence they say: nationality? . . . what country? . . . what country is yours? "Where I make money", I tell them.' He moved about, rubbing his finger on table surfaces, holding glittering ashtrays to the light. Calnan thought of Brennan's malodorous mop, the watches, the ludicrous black eyepiece focused on nothing.

Ari was saying, 'Everyone stop for a piss at Cyprus. Rome, the Greek, Arabs, Gyppos, Venice, every bastard.' He glanced to see if Calnan was listening. 'And you know this English king, Cal, the one with the lion's heart?'

Calnan nodded.

'He sell it to someone and they sell it to the King of Jerusalem! Good joke, Cal. Have a laugh. You don't have to own it to sell it, see?'

'Like twelve cases of liquor,' Calnan said.

That amused Ari. He sat and laughed for almost a minute, linking piece to piece with what could have been ageless swear-words. 'Everyone come to fight a battle, have a piss and move. But four hundred years of Turk, Cal! That's bad!' He came and said very quietly to Calnan, 'The woman, child, they send for slaves. The man?' Ari pulled a finger across his throat. 'Thousands, twenty, thirty, I don't know. Maybe more. Everywhere a church, the holy place, burned, pulled down to nothing. The Turk! And now he's back again! You know a country like that, Cal, you tell me!'

'A most distressful country,' Calnan said. He paid Ari for the food. 'Ring Morgan,' he said.

Ari nodded.

Sunday morning streets had been empty but for perhaps an unexpected bus, a scuttling taxi, sending faint sounds to a hundred thousand grinding bedrooms and tests of love. There was a stir now, a half an hour before midday. A half an hour to pub-time. Calnan left the beaten tracks that Neelan or Mackessy might take. He went by Stoke Newington Church Street, Clissold Park, crossed Green Lanes and passed the Catholic church and the great football field on his route to Holloway. By the railway there was a music-pub he hadn't visited for years. The food, the Metaxa, Ari's great defence of loneliness, the escaping bouzouki notes, had somehow, for a while at least, brought a warm perspective. He found the pub, fading and decrepit, like Ari's island passing from hand to hand, demeaned in the squalid snatch of profit and loss. You earned money and spent it, Calnan thought. Buying money, selling money, was a guttersnipe game.

He bought a drink and found a seat, nodded to recognition here and there. The musicians were on a podium of beer-crates and filthy chipboard, tuning, frowning, worrying about nuances; all of them smoked, took deep draughts from pint tumblers, waiting for some moment of decision. Suddenly they were playing and Calnan looked deep into his glass, almost breathless with the memory of it. His own music. For an instant, just an instant, conversation leaped an octave. Some primeval brotherhood took shape. A slow air brought silence like a web on the house and sudden leaps into rhythm set off roars like battle-cries. Calnan could remember sparks flying from steel tips on flagged kitchen floors, musicians on sugawns, the oil lamps, the flare of turf and bog-deal from the hearth. He had sat on the unguarded steps to a loft, watching, listening, a long time ago.

At two o'clock the music ceased, the men of home and method took their leave, the strays and mavericks and Calnan sat on behind barred doors and curtains drawn. The bar was almost in darkness. Someone sent Calnan a drink and he raised his glass to where it might have come from. A man was singing, muted, out of sight, and the call went from singer to singer. The songs were all of tears and anger, hardly a smile or compassion anywhere. Calnan supposed that Ari too, in the shadow of the Turk, would sing less of love than of war.

At four-thirty he took a mini-cab to the Trade Winds, sat on in the passenger seat and sent the driver to rouse the mourners. Morgan, impassive, nodded from the window, a mask of reassurance: all was well. Brennan came first, a credit to the decorum of his fruitful spouse: a white starched shirt, a black tie, a hat; but only polished shoes and oiled heads distinguished mourners Neelan and Mackessy from their day-to-day visage.

'We were worried,' Neelan said.

'Not about the hour,' Mackessy explained. 'In case there might have been a balls-up, a mishap, accident, that kind of thing. Amazing how misfortunes keep each other company.'

Sitting in the rear, they felt somehow a need to shout, as if over a long distance.

'There isn't room to fart in this meat-box,' Neelan said.

'Make sure you don't,' Calnan said.

'You want to walk, uncle, I'll put you down,' the sensitive driver said.

But they were already in Upper Street. Calnan paid. The door of Canonbury Chapels of Rest opened magically, slowly, with dignity, and the Clincher offered his reverential smile.

'Cal, gentlemen, my condolences on this sad occasion. Come in, won't you?'

Brennan was agog with the simple nobility of the Clincher. 'Good of you,' he said.

The Clincher bowed.

'How are things on the Coal Quay?' Neelan said in passing. 'Drippin'-toast, pigs'-feet and packet high on the menu. A piss in the Lee for afters.'

Mackessy's face was blank as an idiot's.

'You laid in a bottle for me?' Calnan said.

'Of course.'

The Clincher locked and barred his door: he guided them behind his counter in the feeble light seeping in from the pavements: the brass and brown was flat as a canvas without depth. The girlie books and remnants of indulgence were gone, Calnan noted. The blotter was snow-white and a black Bible sat like a bird on a nest. The Clincher ushered them into the privacy of his office: his desk, deep purple carpet, in a corner a wrought-iron standard lamp, warm, discreet; there were books, a Dali crucifixion print, the Lord's Prayer elegantly framed, an expensive gas fire and yet another crucifix on its polished surround. The Clincher's desk had its own little pool of light, its books of business, a cigarette box, a decanter of pale sherry. He motioned them to chairs of leather and heavy brass studding and sat, suitably composed, in his swivel chair to survey them. He noted Neelan's glare, a rictus of contempt or derision for the sherry decanter.

'Waterford,' the Clincher said, touching it gently. 'I only have special people in here. A glass of sherry is a courteous gesture. The English are reserved in their grief. Stoical, you might say, shunning even drink. They sip it in acknowledgment of course but mostly leave it there.'

'And you can tip it back in the Waterford jam jar,' Neelan said.

Mackessy nodded. 'It improves with age.'

The Clincher smiled indulgently at the drollery. From a cabinet in his desk he took a bottle of Hennessy and balloon glasses. 'Compliments of Mr Calnan. Perhaps you'd like to pour?' he said, choosing Brennan.

Brennan glowed before the Clincher's esteem. He poured civilised measures in the glasses and was about to distribute them when Neelan dispossessed him. 'You're not flying with canaries, Flip-flop!' he said; he emptied the bottle carefully, evenly, into the five glasses and left them for the picking. Brennan served Calnan and the Clincher.

'Lord have mercy on the dead,' Brennan said and gratefully caught the Clincher's nod of approval. They drank.

'You're like a judge behind that desk,' Mackessy said. 'A judge looking down at your courtroom.'

'An interesting point of view.' The Clincher smiled.

'More familiar from this end,' Neelan said. 'From the dock, eh, Clincher?'

'If you say so,' the Clincher allowed: the slight lilt of his origins enhanced his dignity, had a faint echo of honesty. He nodded again to Brennan. 'We wish the soul of Mr Davis the joy of Heaven.'

Calnan drank.

'Duffy,' Brennan amended gently, 'James Duffy.'

The Clincher continued. 'May it rest in peace, the soul of your cherished colleague, Mr Davis.'

'Duffy!' Neelan said. 'James Duffy, for Christ's sake!'

'James William Duffy.' Mackessy was stumbling into amusement.

Neelan caught the spirit. 'You're burying the wrong man, you dressed-up fart!'

The Clincher was calm as a summer pond, only the slightest creasing of his face at the jangle of laughter. He held a finger aloft. 'Gentlemen, not a burial, you understand. A cremation.'

'Yes,' Brennan said in defence of the Clincher, his flawless champion. 'A little respect, gentlemen.'

'Close down, Flip-flop,' Mackessy told him.

'You could sell him a watch,' Neelan said. 'He doesn't know what day it is!'

From a silence Brennan said shrewdly, 'Or how many names had Duffy.'

Calnan had sat a little behind the storm-troopers, had sipped

107

his brandy; now, he exhaled noisily, shifted his chair, made a silence for the Clincher.

'Let us see,' the Clincher said, prayer-like, opening his ledger. '"Roderick Hodder O'Callaghan Davis."' He quietly recited the brief history of Duffy's passing and said finally, '"DOA, Whittington Casualty." Dead on arrival, that is, gentlemen. Accompanied by . . .' He looked at them. '"Henry Neelan. Thomas Mackessy."'

There was a little silence. Neelan said, 'You're on to something, Clincher boy. There's a bundle somewhere. You're a dodgy bastard.'

The Clincher laughed politely. 'Duffy, as Mr Brennan mentioned, was probably an alias. One of several perhaps. Run of the mill in hospital morgues. We amended it at his cousin's request.'

'Elmer Devine,' Neelan said.

'Ah, you know him?'

'Do you know him?' Neelan said.

'A perfect gentleman.' The Clincher was creating him. 'Sitting just where you are. American. State of Alabama. Tall, greying at the temples, a beard not quite hiding a scar . . .'

Calnan was suddenly remembering his taxi spin to the hospital, the courteous, vanishing driver he had forgotten, never mentioned to the Clincher; the beard, the scar . . .

'And you passed him the second-hand sherry,' Mackessy said, but less sure of himself now.

'He found it excellent,' the Clincher said. 'He gave me lunch and took me to the hospital. He had a chauffeured Daimler. And he identified Roderick Hodder O'Callaghan Davis of course.' The Clincher closed his book. 'Down to a childhood fracture of the right femur, that's his thigh, and a slight deformity of the toes.'

The Sunday six o'clock traffic outside, distant, came in little irregular disturbances of relief: the mandatory visits to the sick, the dying or ageing forebears, were at an end and the sweet relief of the visited was to have silence again. Soon only the pubs and the Pakis would be open. Neelan took half a bottle of brandy from his pocket, poured himself a long greedy measure and blindly held the bottle out for takers. The Clincher laid a palm across his glass, Calnan's face was a refusal; but Mackessy enlisted – one would have thought, without enthusiasm – and left hardly a dribble for Brennan.

'The personal effects?' Mackessy said in a hopeless attempt to upstage the Clincher. 'Less than a couple of quid and a busted watch! That's crap! And who's this executor we hear about?'

'I haven't the slightest idea,' the Clincher said. 'These are family matters. I finalise dozens of bereavements – burials, cremations – in the space of a month, rule off my accounts and meet the next grief-stricken face at my door. No more.' The Clincher turned to Calnan. 'Executors advertise the winding-up of affairs.'

'Local papers,' Calnan nodded.

'If you owed money to the deceased or were indebted in any way,' the Clincher said to Neelan, 'you can make restitution to the executor.'

Neelan paled. 'There could have been five ton in his bloody jock-strap!' he bellowed at him.

And in the moments of silence that followed Brennan mumbled in apology. 'His underpants . . . underclothes.'

'Casualty departments,' the Clincher said, 'meet a variety of unsavoury nether garments in cases of DOA. A quick dash to the incinerator, I'm afraid.'

Calnan wondered at the polish of the Clincher, the astuteness: he was impregnable. And the strange picture of Elmer Devine? From his own brandy bottle he poured a drink and warmed it in his hands. He nodded towards the Clincher.

'Good health,' the Clincher said. 'It's a poor choice of subject, gentlemen. Sordid, distressing.'

'Rich pickings for the grave-robbers,' Mackessy fired off.

The Clincher considered it. 'All human depravities are in practice at any given moment,' he said; and with a great deal of sympathy counselled Neelan, 'It's your duty, you realise, to tender this information to the police. If you're sure.' He laid a hand on a deep grey telephone. 'I could get them for you.'

'I wouldn't dirty my hands groping in the same crawling thunder-box. Christ!' he said. 'The corpse-blockers, the filth, the little mortuary maggots!'

A black telephone on the Clincher's desk rang. He raised it and listened. 'A little later, my dear,' he said. 'I have one or two special people here.' He gently replaced it. 'My wife. We like to watch the money programme on Sundays,' he explained. 'Our home is in Mill Hill,' he said to Neelan. 'Very big and with the children at boarding-school my wife finds it lonely at times. Understandable. Mr Elmer Devine sent her a bouquet yesterday. Roses in November. Cheered her up a great deal.' He tidied and arranged his desk. 'You could pay your respects to Mr Davis now, if you wish.'

'He came from America, did he, Clincher?'

The Clincher pondered. 'Elmer Devine?'

'Andy Devine. Buster Crabbe, the Three Stooges, whoever he is!'

'Alabama,' Brennan tried to explain.

Neelan ignored him, took a careful bead on the Clincher. 'How did he know Duffy was dead?'

Mackessy was suddenly restored, Brennan in doubt; Calnan awaited the vagaries of the plot.

'Davis. Roderick Hodder O'Callaghan Davis,' the Clincher corrected him.

'How did Elmer Devine know that Duffy was dead?' Neelan dropped each word like a stone in a deep pond. 'Duffy, Davis or Johnnie the Ragman?'

'A very strange business,' the Clincher said immediately. 'Disturbing in fact.' He forestalled all interruption by standing to address them. 'Gentlemen, you could say that death is my business. I live with death. Beside us here, in our Chapels of Rest, we have the human tabernacles from which souls have

110

fled. Eight of them, gentlemen. Call them bodies if you like, cadavers, corpses, whatever. But, gentlemen, I believe that beside each one stands a dead soul keeping a vigil with its remains. When you visit Mr Davis, in a few moments, remember you are being watched.' He stopped and seemed to listen. 'We are not alone now in this room. I can feel it. And I have stood in there in the small hours,' he looked towards the Chapels of Rest, 'and heard them breathing. Yes, breathing. Even laughing. I have come on their faces and felt that only a moment before they were creased in amusement. Souls and bodies, like old friends, part reluctantly.' There was stillness now. The Clincher sipped a little brandy. A two-stroke motor cycle came and went like a demented lawn mower. 'Mr Elmer Devine,' the Clincher said as if announcing his entrance, 'was called upon to come. Called upon.' He allowed an adequate silence. 'He was driving, it seems, in downtown Montgomery where his business interests are considerable, when the familiar street disappeared beneath his wheels and suddenly it was night-time in an old mouldering city. There was a man lying on the broad pavement and two strange gaping figures standing over him.'

'Gaping?' Calnan said.

'Two strange gaping figures,' the Clincher confirmed. 'It lasted only moments and instantly it was daytime again in his own crowded streets. He knew at that instant that cousin Roderick had passed over. He came at once.'

'He wasted no time,' Brennan agreed. 'It must be a fair step to Montgomery.'

'He flew,' the Clincher said and forestalled Neelan. 'In a plane, gentlemen? Perhaps not. One must know when it is indelicate to pry.'

'But he paid you?' Mackessy said with belligerence almost sapped, a tone of unease stealing his volume. 'In real money?'

'In dollars. And then left so suddenly I didn't see him go.' The Clincher remembered it. 'Hundred-dollar bills, banked and receipted. "Ten Cs should cover it", he said. "Adequately", I told him.'

Neelan was faltering now; he took a reserve half-bottle from Mackessy's pocket, poured himself a measure, ignored the company.

'He disappeared?'

'Yes.'

'Like that!'

'Exactly.'

'Is there a strong family resemblance?' Neelan asked eventually.

'Hardly,' the Clincher said. 'Mr Elmer Devine is a Negro.'

'Jesus!' Neelan said. 'Spades in the Duffys!'

A courteous Negro, Calnan thought.

'He was a psychic cousin, you understand,' the Clincher said. 'I think you'll find that Mr Davis . . . Mr Duffy, as you call him . . . was close to the spirit world.'

Brennan crossed himself. 'Is Mr Duffy . . . Mr Davis here now?' he whispered.

'Perhaps,' the Clincher said. 'But Mr Devine is here. I can feel his presence.' He closed his book, pondered, nodded sympathetically at no one in particular.

Calnan was remembering the magnifying glass, mint sweets, coloured girlie spreads, the crossword awaiting the final links. The Clincher would be at home with white-haired old spectres winding clocks on wild November evenings, he thought. The room had been silent for a whole minute or more. Yes, Calnan thought, the Clincher was a fine performer.

Calnan said, 'I think we should pay our respects to the deceased now.'

The Clincher nodded. He led them through the outer reception space to the door of the black and gold-leaf motel of the dead. The 'chapels' were tastefully dressed stables: a line of doorless stables, each with its catafalque, four electric candles on helical brass standards, a prie-dieu, a Bible, artificial greenery rounding the angles.

Brennan 'froze' in the doorway.

'Have no fear,' the Clincher told him. 'You have a great aura of peace about you. You seem to be welcome here.' The polished parquet blocks shone in reassurance. The air was cold. From each coffin folded waxen hands and faces, all chin and nostrils, caught the faint light and reflected it. The Clincher led, the trio stalked as if stealing upon birds, and Calnan, behind, paused to look at a young man with pale Christ-like hair; and a little further on, a great dignified matriarch with long fingers anchored to precious beads. Perhaps each one, a sentinel, was standing there in contemplation before the take-off, awaiting the burning, the burial. At Duffy's chapel the Clincher halted them, switched on the electric candles to throw a kindly light on the thin face, peeved even in death, and hands unsullied by work. The silence seemed total behind insulated walls and doors. Neelan, Mackessy, Brennan, glanced from the corpse to the coffin's perimeter, to its headboard, in search of a disembodied Duffy.

Calnan said very softly, 'Well, if he's standing there, we wish him Godspeed.' He turned and led the way out; they were pushing against him, against each other, in their urgency.

'You'll excuse me if I don't join you for a drink next door,' the Clincher said. 'I'll get back to Mill Hill. A number of disposals tomorrow. A heavy day.'

'Of course,' Brennan said: fear and admiration were battling for supremacy; in a few minutes his hands had paled in the still mortuary.

Neelan stamped his feet, Mackessy pulled his coat about him.

'Christ!' Neelan said. 'It's a deep freeze in there.'

'Perishing,' Mackessy said.

'Oh, not cold surely,' the Clincher smiled. 'Ten Celsius the year round. Constant. Good for the quick and the dead.' He looked to Calnan.

'I didn't notice,' Calnan said.

113

The Clincher nodded. 'As it should be.' He paused and looked at Neelan. 'Of course, a restless presence, it's said, can breathe cold on its quarry. A kind of desperate manifestation.'

'Presence?' Neelan said.

The Clincher walked to the pavement door with them. 'A spirit,' he explained to Neelan. 'An unquiet spirit.' The door clicked shut on his placid face, on a houseful of corpses suspended in reverence.

In the pub, Mackessy said, 'God in heaven, I feel dirty. The light was dirty in there, it seemed to stick.' He rubbed his hands, his face.

Brennan nodded. 'It takes an iron man to stand a job like that, day in, day out. Bodies coming and going. People breaking down in sorrow.'

'Well, we spared him that,' Calnan said.

The black epiphany of Elmer Devine, the Archway Road suddenly a death scene in downtown Montgomery, spirits, presences, the cold breath of unrest, a disembodied Duffy watching over his shell, all crowded their anxious fugitive thoughts. Neelan had been shaken but a great vindictive anger was rising in defence.

He said, 'There's something evil about that oily ponce.' He gestured at the bright reality of the pub, bottles, people, a growing noise. 'The unquiet spirit hawing cold air on his quarry! Christ, what's that about?'

'Not a quarry where you break stones,' Brennan explained. 'The fox on the run from the hounds, that kind of thing . . .'

'When we have cleaning problems we'll send for you!' Neelan snapped.

'Or a turbo Mickey Mouse watch with an airlock.' Mackessy's anger had roots in uncertainty too.

'I can't see any reason,' Calnan said thoughtfully, 'why Duffy's spirit should be unquiet. He was surrounded by friends.' Neelan was searching Calnan's face for humour but Calnan seemed to drift and capitulate to the unknown. 'A strange business,' he said.

Neelan whispered, 'You don't believe that sheep–shagger, do you?' He scoffed at the whimsy. 'Some black Batman from Alabama peeling off hundred–dollar bills and Duffy on guard duty in his Chapel of Rest! A converted fish and chipper! You don't believe that crap, do you?'

Eventually when Calnan said, 'I keep an open mind,' it had all the weight of a thunderous affirmative. 'Your own family?' Calnan remembered. 'Your father, God rest him, exploding light bulbs in the toilet.'

'Duffy,' Brennan decided. 'We'll get a novena of Masses said for the peace of his soul.'

'What are you talking about?' Mackessy asked him.

'Nine Masses to lay his spirit at rest.'

'You're talking about twenty–five or thirty pounds!'

'The missus will do the sandwiches for nothing.' Brennan blessed himself with unsteady hands, inadvertently upset Neelan's glass so that brandy dripped like a libation of penitence.

'You're an awkward bollicks,' Neelan told him.

Calnan said, 'I have a call to make.' He put a fiver on the counter. 'You can knock that out.'

'Without much trouble,' Mackessy mumbled.

'We should be back at the Trade Winds, not stamping our feet here,' Brennan said; he pointed. 'Behind that wall, twenty feet away, eight corpses are lying in the dark. It puts a taste on the liquor.'

Calnan prepared to leave.

'I have a call to make myself,' Neelan announced. 'About nine. An hour or so should cover it. I'll make it back to base, say ten.'

Calnan could see Mackessy was in the dark, hardly hiding curiosity, suspicion.

'A bit of exhibition work in the offing,' Neelan said. 'I must see a man. Not too many can make it into that field, you see. You can call your price. Brandies!' he said to a passing barman and tapped Calnan's fiver. 'I suppose you want a drink?' he asked Brennan and called out, 'That's three brandies, cocker!'

'Don't forget the exhibition work on my bathroom,' Calnan said. 'That'll be number one.' He left them and caught a taxi at Highbury Corner.

The beautiful slender houses, doors, fanlights, windows, of ageing, rambling Georgian times flitted past: iron-railed basement areas, worn doorsteps and shoe-scrapers. Canonbury Tower had Tudor carving, huge open hearths, a haunted room, had housed Bacon and Spencer and who else? It sat in its precious garden, listening to the hush and rush of its theatre. Calnan liked to sit there sometimes when Restoration larks of style and bawd and foppery were played. He seemed to belong in them.

He paid off his taxi at Cassie's door and rang and stood in the shadow of its embrasure, looking obliquely at the warm windows of the Trade Winds. Cassie's voice came through the speaker, he answered and the door swung open. He drank long and steadily from his bottle, leant back against the door until it clicked shut.

In the hallway, beneath the soffit of the stairs was a broom cupboard, large enough for Calnan to stand inside its door in hiding; there was a narrow flight of stairs to a landing where, on a waist-high pedestal, a rubber plant sprouted from a brass pot; beyond that, the stairs turned away to Cassie's maisonette.

Calnan was checking his stage, his props. He looked at the door behind him and saw that Cassie had left the return-spring in abeyance.

'Everything OK?' she called down to him.

'Fine.'

She was waiting for him in her doorway; a picture, Calnan thought, in a Chinese kimono housecoat, pale pink with gold and green, a splash of chrysanthemums, belled sleeves, skirt as broad as a crinoline.

She brought him a bottle and a warm glass, a shining

116

goblet, drank orange juice to keep him company. Calnan's
recital of the afternoon's progress jumped in and out of farce;
he found himself smiling at the outrageous nonsense of players
and play.

'I'll fix him,' she said.

The room was a warm crowded palace of music, posters,
prints, a thousand paperbacks, pewter, crystal glass and a single
flamboyant house-plant thriving in the midst of carnival. And
there was a photograph of Lakeland.

'I have a house there,' she told Calnan. 'A little house.
October is my month. I like it with summer out of sight and
just the odd blow of winter.'

Calnan was looking at the deep shadows of morning and
the first weak light netted in the mist. He nodded to her. He
thought of the day growing older and spirals of mist rising up
from the glass sheen of water.

'Anytime you want the keys, just ask,' she was saying: it
was a gift she could always share with her friends. Except
October. 'The peace, Cal. I bring whodunnits and music,
that's all. I sit for bloody hours and watch and listen. And if it
rains or storms I can wrap up like a fisherman, be blown and
pelted along the sheep-tracks.' She topped up Calnan's glass.
'As pure, Cal,' she said, 'as a whore on a holiday!' She stood,
orange juice in hand, laughing at Calnan's sudden bark of
amusement. 'But Christmas, I go to Brighton. They like to
see me. They're getting old.'

'Like me.'

'More than that,' she said. 'And very old in here.' She
tapped Calnan's chest. 'Don't forget the Lakes. Except
October.'

Time didn't loiter in Cassie's domain; she seemed to sweep
it out with every word and smile and movement. Doors
opened to her bedroom and to a kitchen where Calnan would
spend his moments of enforced voyeurism. The trap was laid.

'You never married?' she said.

'No.'

117

'Or thought of it?'

Calnan laughed. 'Over the sticks was as near as I wanted. Afraid, girl. When I could bull I was broke. Now I'm heeled, I'm hamstrung. Glad of it too. An old bull in grope and scramble wouldn't be my style.' He held up his glass for inspection, spun the golden liquor. 'This "lassie" is fine. Outlived, no bawling when I go.'

'No,' she smiled to him. 'It wouldn't be your style, Cal.'

The doorbell rang on the dot of nine. 'Yes?' she said in her speaker and the voice below, sounding so pretty, came back. 'This is Harry. Harry Neelan.'

'Harry, darling, come right up.'

Calnan, glass in hand, was on his way to the kitchen. She winked to him as he closed the door and shut himself off. It was a used kitchen, cared for, important – even copper pans – and it smelt of fruit and baked bread. The space of an outside fitted mirror was the coign of vantage: he could sit on a high kitchen stool by Cassie's neat rack of herbs and spices, and command the living-room. He watched her switch on what must be some proven therapeutic music, he imagined, but no sound came to him. Like the Clincher's Chapels of Rest, it was a place of silence.

She met Neelan at the door with a quick huge pouting kiss that dumbfounded him and a dallying flick of her fingers in his crotch. Calnan, in his silence, imagined a sudden swarm of disturbed horse-flies. Neelan was crouched in the doorway, like a bathing belle defending her honour, and doubt already in his face of his ability to maintain such speed and performance.

Cassie closed the door, led him like a schoolboy to the table and poured a bumper drink. Before he could raise it she had put her arms about his neck and was clinging to him as if pulled in by some overpowering vacuum. When she released him he gawped for a moment and dived for the brandy. He drank half of it. She kissed her finger, put it on his lips, smiled, winked, drifted away to her bedroom just long enough for the brandy to be gulped and another one pinched. Neelan drank from the bottle too. The ebb of courage had ended, the tide was on the turn; he looked about at the colour and joy that surrounded him. Cassie returned, dimmed her lights, sat demurely beside him. He raised his glass to her. From a console she switched on for them a pulsing video and lay against him, fingering his limp thinning hair.

Calnan watched the video with a deal of surprise, even wonder: every pubescent invention of bondage and possession, of savagery, was realised; but there was a sickness of raw meat and decay that lessened them all. He drank from his glass and his bottle and felt cleaner. He would never find the key to God's mixture of innocence and amorality that, for Cassie, a whole world, found love in laying, beauty in porno, good in everything. But he liked them all.

Neelan-aroused was coming to life now, maddened with licence, beginning to wrestle. The video ended with the suddenness of death. Cassie disentangled herself, kissed him on the cheek, started him on the impatient eternity of un-dressing. She went to stand in the lighted frame of her bedroom door, her back to his modesty, and let the kimono drop from her shoulders.

It was almost time. Neelan in nakedness was a capering deformed goat: like a Burmese dancer he raised each leg hip-high, knee bent, for perhaps the release of a great nervous flatulence or even some arcane trick of virility; and then in a last moment of decency he clamped a shirt over his manhood as if hiding a terrible injury. Cassie whisked him inside, shut the door.

It took Calnan less than thirty seconds to rifle Neelan's pockets: he took everything that was money, even small change, and, leaving the door open, moved downstairs. He dropped Neelan's coat and trousers on the landing, kicked the pedestal from under the rubber plant, sent the brass pot clattering like a broken bell from step to step. He heard Cassie's scream, a confusion of feet. He hurried down to open the street door wide and turned back to slip into hiding beneath the stairs.

There was little in the pitch or decibels to distinguish the twin yells of outrage from above.

'My coat, my suit!'

'My jewels!' Cassie sent spearing through it.

Neelan's bare feet slithered on the landing. 'My coat! My suit! Jesus, I'm robbed!'

A sweeping-brush makes a hollow clubbing sound when it strikes masonry and a dull thud against flesh and bone. Cassie missed on the first swing, Calnan read; the second brought a whingeing screech of pain and terror. 'You set me up, you bastard! Left the door open, didn't you!'

Rhythmically, as she called out, 'My jewels, my jewels, my jewels!' she hammered him. Calnan knew from the hopping dancing tempo of Neelan that, trousers gripped, he was, leg-in, leg-out, struggling for modesty, roaring in pain, the cataclysmic explosion of loss only moments away.

They were at Calnan's level now, in the hallway.

'You robbed me, you brasser, you hoor! A dead man's whip! You hoor!'

'A dead man's dick!' Cassie yelled at him and from Neelan's whistling whoop of torment, she had twirled the broom-handle, kendo style, to catch his tenderest parts on the upswing.

He was saying, 'You thieving hoor . . .' but midway it tapered off to a single quavering thread of shock.

'Out! Out!'

Calnan heard the last thump as Neelan crossed the threshold and the clatter of his shoes as Cassie pitched them in his wake.

The door slammed shut.

In a few moments Calnan emerged still wearing the strain of his harsh merriment, hand raised in approbation. Cassie, modest, virtuous, in her housecoat of pink and green and gold, squatted down and kept vigil from the letter-box.

'Between parked cars,' she relayed.

120

'Getting his shoes on?'

'Right. Collar up now, he's on the move.'

'The Trade Winds?'

She nodded and came to sit on the stairs below Calnan. 'You got it?'

'Everything.' He held out a note. 'We owe you ten.'

She smiled.

'I must buy you a nice present when we see the end of Duffy,' he said. 'Something special. Something for that house near the Lakes.'

They sat in silence, Cassie glowing in the aftermath of battle. But Calnan was thinking of Mackessy, the unrecovered loot.

He counted Neelan's roll and wondered what Mackessy held and how he might get it. They could hear the soft endless music left flowing upstairs.

Calnan hauled himself up; Cassie reconnoitred the desolate Sunday street and signalled him out. She blew him a kiss.

9

Calnan stood on the pavement for a few moments. The road was still quiet, swept of people and traffic: late Sunday, the fag-end of the week. In a couple of hours the fifty-tonners would roll again, the old loose windows would tremble with the vibrancy of a drill. Another week.

It would be an hour before Morgan had cleared, had hung wet towels on the pumps and Brennan had snailed from ashtray to ashtray and left the wet smear of a dirty swab behind him. Upstairs, there was light in the bathroom too: that would be Neelan squatting by the rubble, penniless, in shock.

Calnan turned down a narrow alley, the width of a car perhaps, guarded at each end by cast-iron Victorian bollards. It was still paved with granite sets and a waste and storm-water channel bisected it. It was a little canyon; the walls that he could almost reach with outstretched arms had been houses, two-up-two-down, but now had blind bricked-up doors and windows. People had lived there once, looking into each other's kitchens, throwing slops, and soil waste too, into the open channel: but even in hot days they were insulated from the fetid smell of their lives.

Bombs had fallen where the high-rise tenements now spiked up, and people locked their doors, and the urine and even excrement was on the awful neglected stairways. People were a bloody nuisance. Calnan smiled with no humour at all.

In an open space he sat on a bulky horizontal tree trunk,

looked about at a gantry of swinging ropes, a scaffolding frame, scattered concrete pipes for children to crawl through, a quirky sign inviting them to adventure.

The dark enfolded Calnan in a great stillness. He became aware that the wind had dropped and it was less cold; the stars lay beyond a blanket of cloud. Not even a dog barked, he thought; and he remembered lying in his loft bedroom, all that lifetime ago, listening to wind that must have rubbed against the rushes and black bog-lake and the crosses and mounds of graveyards to set up such a constant thread of keening: dogs barking to each other across the night then were howls of relief, a reassurance that light would come again.

He walked away across the wilderness of open space and litter, the planned gardens and greenery lost in a dust bowl of tower blocks. It was almost at midnight when he had back-tracked to the Trade Winds. The bar was in darkness but light still shone from the bathroom window. Morgan had seen his shadow on the glass and, as he reached it, the door was opened for him; Morgan's staff had long since gone and the bar was an empty gloom except for Mackessy and Brennan, drinking beer now, at the counter.

'A long day,' Calnan said. 'I should rest.'

'Ari rang.'

'All right?'

'All right.' Morgan was looking towards the pair at the counter, a trace of humour on his bared teeth.

Mackessy was the first down from his stool. 'Neelan's up there! The bathroom. He could be dead. The door locked. No sound. A seizure, maybe!'

'He might be clearing the rubbish,' Calnan said, looking at Brennan.

'But it's like the grave up there,' Brennan said.

Mackessy was mumbling. 'That Clincher bastard has the evil eye.' And then suddenly his spleen was turned on Morgan. 'I told you to force the door!' he said. 'A three-inch runner.

One push!' He saw Calnan's expressionless face. 'Damage made good . . . damage made good, no sweat!'

'He's having a crap,' Morgan said; he moved off to get Calnan a beer.

'A two and a half hour crap!' Mackessy held out his palms to Calnan. 'Two hours and a half, dear Christ!'

'He carries a heavy load,' Morgan said.

Brennan, unable to hide a glowing inner happiness, logged it for Calnan. 'Exhibition work, he says, back at the pub, and he's off! That's Upper Street, half-eight on the boozer clock, and the fiver knocked out. Half-nine, head down, collar up, like a dosser in the rain, he's through that door and upstairs!'

'Coming up for twelve now!' Mackessy pushed out like a challenge to Calnan.

'Who was "the man"? The exhibition work?' Calnan asked him.

Brennan snickered. 'He doesn't know,' he said, feeding a great thirst of resentment. 'Neelan's the gaffer, he's the lad!'

Calnan raised a finger for silence, eyed them without affection for a few moments. Behind them, in deep shadow, Morgan sat, rum in hand. Calnan drank from his beer, glanced at the nicotined skin of the ceiling. 'Wait,' he told them. 'Wait here.'

'I'm afraid I must insist, guv'nor.' Mackessy was in revolt. 'I should be present at a time like this.'

A little silence and Calnan said, 'You'll wait like I told you.' There was no doubt about it.

'Can I buy a drink?' Mackessy said in retreat.

Calnan nodded. 'For the house. One for the craftsman up-stairs too.'

'The crap-man,' Morgan said and Mackessy mouthed something about valleys and goats; and Morgan's amusement was raw spirit on his wounds.

Calnan climbed the stairs and on the landing said very calmly, 'Neelan, I want you down in the bar in three minutes. Don't bring me up again like a good man.'

He went back down and took his drink from Morgan. The gas fire made its steaming sound and wind in the chimney tussled with the flue. Morgan went back to the shadows.

Mackessy said, 'Well?'

'Well what?'

'Did he speak to you?'

'I didn't ask him to.'

In the stillness they heard the creak of Calnan's private door, almost soundless footsteps on the carpet, and from the shadows Neelan emerged, fully dressed, pale as a ticket-of-leave man, a bruise like an ugly hillock on one cheek-bone, skinned knuckles drying dark. He walked in short steps, one hand in his pocket; no doubt, Calnan thought, supporting his upended testicles. Mackessy could hardly find sufficient breath or profanity for amazement to ride on. He rushed to him with a drink.

'You'll have to brush up on the footwork for the next exhibition,' Morgan said.

Mackessy bridled. 'Do us a favour,' he said to Calnan. 'Keep barmen where they belong. Behind counters.'

'Manager,' Calnan said; and then to Neelan, 'Who did you upset this time?'

Neelan was bruised and with both hands he brought the brandy to his lips: he would milk his injuries and shock and outrage now to muffle the disclosures that lay ahead. Loss. Real uncounterfeited loss!

'Give him a chance,' Mackessy said: he was peering at the facial bruise, the raw knuckles. Neelan took the brandy in one drink as if it had the blandness of thin weekend plonk.

'I could do with another one,' Neelan said.

'A brandy!' Mackessy clicked his fingers for Morgan.

Morgan came to him. 'Money?' he said. 'It saves a journey.' And waited for Mackessy to part. Calnan was in the shadows now. 'A drink, guv'nor?'

'Put me in.'

'I'll try one too,' Breenan said.

125

'Jesus! Who makes the suits round here?' Mackessy said, 'Chubbs?'

Neelan stirred uneasily.

'And one for the barman,' Morgan said. 'You'll need a bigger flag than that.' He waited for Mackessy's tenner and went on his way.

'Neelan?' Calnan said from the shadows. 'Can you hear me?'

'I can,' Neelan said eventually as if murmuring through a veil of pain.

'What happened?'

'Mugged,' Neelan said; he seemed to wait for the arrival of strength. 'Three yobbos, maybe four.'

'Darkies?' Brennan asked.

'Balaclavas, like terrorists. Black, white, brown, I couldn't tell you.'

Mackessy was well ahead, racing through a maze of plot, eliminating blind alleys: he was cautious, ruthless as an assassin; he saw not an injured heroic Neelan anymore, but a trick-o'-the-loop man, slick as himself. Slicker. Calnan watched for the flicker of communication between them: it came and went without reassurance. The fingers of Mackessy's hand, by his side, trembled a little.

Calnan said, 'The money?'

'Gone.'

'How much?'

'Down to the last copper.'

'How much?'

Mackessy shouted, whispered. 'The lot! . . . the lot!' His glass, by intent or in shock, shattered against the brick surround of the fireplace. 'The lot, O Christ!' He found the edge of a chair to rest on, eyes riveted on Neelan.

'You were carrying half,' Calnan told Neelan.

'Not since lunchtime!' Mackessy clicked like a slamming door. If Neelan's half could disappear by design or vicissitude so could Mackessy's. No loopholes. Glibness, but steel too,

Calnan could see. 'You weren't here,' Mackessy said. 'The last whip, we tidied up, made one roll of it.'

Calnan said to Neelan, 'You had it? You had it all?'

Neelan nodded; he could read the hovering search for treachery in Mackessy's eyes. Unbearable. Calnan watched them from the shadows. Neelan would take the brickbats, silent or otherwise now, until there was a moment to put Mackessy straight; and, deep down, there must be admiration for the nimbleness of Mackessy. A master stroke. Now there was no whip. Dipped, mugged, set upon. The blameless.

'An unfortunate business,' Calnan said.

For an instant Neelan saw himself naked, fleeing before the swipes of the little thieving whore across the way and the ignominy of it returned so that he crouched and the broomhandle seemed to hammer again against the sanctity of his groin. And the comforting lump of money was gone from his pocket. He groaned.

'Are you all right?' Mackessy said with a total lack of compassion, objective as a field surgeon.

'Sore,' Neelan croaked. 'I took a bad kicking. One in the nuts too. Christ! I had to fight for the punters' money!'

The punters were on a long shot, Calnan thought. 'How much?' he said.

'Including my own, call it three and a half ton.'

'O God!' Brennan said in shock.

'The punks on Saturday,' Mackessy said suddenly to Calnan. 'The dips. They don't forget a clatter in the teeth. That kind of thing can call down vengeance.' Calnan felt the vague breath of censure, the tenuous but unmistakable thread of involvement. 'Arguments are better settled without blows.'

'It could have been Elmer Devine,' Calnan said. 'He moves in strange ways. Or that unquiet spirit blowing cold air.'

'On his quarry.' Once again Brennan set up a holy sign and hid behind it.

Neelan took the lifeline from Mackessy. 'The punks!' he said in growing confidence. 'You could be on the ball. They

127

had reason enough for another strike. That fellow's jaw could be off the hinges. You hit him a savage blow, Cal. The whole bar heard it. The punks!' he said again, nodding his head as with gathering certainty. 'The punks! I remember now before I hit the deck and the boot went in. Orange and purple!'

'But the balaclavas?' Brennan said.

'Manes at their necks!' Mackessy said, tense, waiting.

'I caught him with a fair hook.' Neelan held out his damaged knuckles. 'And as he spun I saw the purple and orange!'

'A pity you had to take action, Cal,' Mackessy said. 'But that's life. When the man loaded his gun in Sarajevo he couldn't see the poppy-fields of Flanders.'

'No,' Calnan said.

They sat in stillness, the night traffic wasn't rolling yet. The mice were moving early: empty crisp bags crackled in their stops and starts.

'Mice,' Brennan said.

Mackessy nodded. 'Dirt brings them round a place.'

'Could you do us a drink all round?' Neelan asked.

'What will you use for money?' Calnan watched him.

Mackessy was a lifeless shell discarded by its senses; eventually he was restored. 'I polished the mahogany all night,' he said. 'Expensive polish.'

'Your own money too,' Calnan agreed.

Brennan said humbly, 'How far will two quid get me?'

'To the traffic-lights in a mini-cab,' Mackessy told him. 'You should drink in your own league, Flip-flop. You're out of your depth.'

Calnan might have smiled in the shadows; Brennan's disparagement saddened him a little; Morgan, silent so long, said, 'Christ!' and laughed.

Fourteen hours to Duffy's last journey, Calnan thought: he looked and could see the gladness in their faces for such a vague uncharted world.

'Could you chalk me one on the slate, Cal?' Neelan said.

'No.'

Mackessy looked down at his broken glass and brandy almost inhaled by the gas fire. Calnan knew he was fingering the notes in his pocket. Finally he opened his fist on a tenner. 'I can do one more,' he said stonily to Calnan. 'That's it! Tomorrow is someone else's problem!'

Tomorrow! Like a dreaded shibboleth it was uttered at last. Morgan went about the business of drinks and served them. Silence circled like a dog and finally settled.

'Tomorrow,' Calnan said, 'will be a difficult day.'

'Well,' Mackessy said, 'the funeral is paid for.'

Neelan was bearing up with great fortitude. 'And Brennan's old woman is standing the grub. That's two out of three.'

Brennan stood transfixed. 'Masses, I said! Nine Masses to ease his spirit. To calm the dead.'

'Well, we're back to sandwiches now,' Mackessy said. 'To ease the living. Get the missus wound up in the morning. Get out the starting handle.'

Brennan was seized in a moment of panic. 'My missus wouldn't feed staggering birds in the frost!'

'Sandwiches!' Mackessy said and ground him to silence.

Neelan was almost happy now. 'Not bad, not bad. Two out of three.'

Calnan studied him. 'Number three would be "the drink" of course? What had you in mind?'

Neelan sadly contemplated grand schemes agley, his help-lessness before some Olympian brotherhood of mischievous gods. He showed open palms of impotence to Calnan. 'A ton plus in the kitty, we thought. And then every man for himself. A generous farewell.'

'You're in a hole.'

'I know.'

'A lot of men on that list could be very severe about such matters as drink.'

'Look!' Mackessy said; he paced about with a great air of deliberation, astuteness, addressed himself fervently to Calnan.

'I wouldn't have it on my conscience to leave a stain like that on the Trade Winds. God forbid!' He raised his hand for total stillness: a bus came and went, an old hammering car. 'We'll be due a ton when the bathroom is finished. Right?'

Calnan was motionless.

'Put it in the kitty and we're square!'

There was a hush awaiting the thunder of Calnan but he said quietly, 'The bathroom and we're square. Finish your drinks.' He nodded and Morgan came to supervise the tilting of glasses. A warm cloud of relief sat on them and perhaps a trace of victory.

Neelan, with great effort, got to his feet and the light crept slowly along his face until it caught the shiny lump on his cheek-bone; he held the chair with one hand and with the other tenderly on his crotch he seemed to raise himself up.

'Lucky the yobbos were bent,' Morgan said. 'They could have left you dead on the deck like Duffy.'

'What's he gabbling about?' Neelan said.

'The kiss of life, boyo.' Morgan put a finger almost on Neelan's lips and traced the pale pink perimeter of Cassie's lipstick. 'You must have turned them on, boyo! Or did you stop off somewhere for a swift leg-over on the way? Enter of course!'

The working of Mackessy's mind, almost calm and in tune again, jangled at the impact of this fresh spanner; Brennan squinted as if the whole smeared orifice was an indecent exposure.

'Bollicks!' Neelan exploded into the silence, scrubbing at himself, his frightened eyes locked on Morgan. 'There was a fight, you know!'

'A clash of heads.' Morgan smiled unhappily at him, moved off with the glasses.

Mackessy followed him. 'A half-bottle of brandy to carry out, you poisonous bastard,' he said; he sported another ten and rapped his knuckles on the counter. Morgan grinned – white brilliant teeth in the gloom – and served him.

'Come on,' Calnan said but at the door he held them a moment. 'Drink, flowers, a few quid on the heres and theres: the cleric, the corpse-gang, the car-men, all that. There would have been a fair little balance at the bottom of the can.' Calnan seemed to think about it. 'A pity. A very fair balance.'

There was silence and Mackessy bared his rueful smile to the sky, to the street lights. 'It was going to be a surprise,' he said.

'Was it?'

'We know a gardener in the parks at Haringey,' Neelan said.

'A floral artist,' Mackessy interrupted.

Calnan listened; behind a calm credulous visage he wondered at the crackle of imagination and fantasy and what miraculous conflation would emerge. It would be nothing simple, of course. But he gave them a springboard.

'Is he doing the flowers?'

'Funeral stuff! He wouldn't touch that class of work,' Neelan said forgivingly. 'He looks at things and they grow.'

'And,' Mackessy said, 'he knows a carpenter, a joiner.'

'A craftsman,' Calnan helped out. 'The gardener knows a craftsman.'

'Exactly. And he makes the seats in the parks.'

'You're ahead of me now,' Calnan said.

'And me,' Brennan added.

Neelan smiled, patted Brennan's shoulder: there must be no risk of confrontation in matters fiscal. 'All in good time,' he said and deferred to Mackessy.

Mackessy too projected the great human impotence in God's own maze, the fragility of plans, the sadness. 'We had in mind a quiet corner of flowers where the grass and shrubs give shelter. And a plain oak seat, the work of a craftsman, looking out on it all.'

'The inscription,' Neelan said, 'would be carved in the wood – "James Duffy spent many happy hours here".'

'Did he?' Brennan in blankness seemed to see it all.

'Not Thursdays,' Calnan said, closing the door on them. 'Thursdays he did a turn at Stoke Newington.' He came back to Morgan and the fire. 'Get us a good drink, Taff. A good drink.'

'They could have been in the City,' Morgan said. 'The FT index like a darts' raffle with cloakroom tickets.'

'I need a rest. Not a lot but some,' Calnan said; he sat away from the gas fire, stretched his legs towards it, listened to its endless flow. On his travels he thought about the rooms that lay beyond net curtains and imprisoned potted plants; or the imprisoned faces behind modish curtainless windows, surrounded by books and etchings and little spills of light, gods in their universes to be gazed on and envied; a world of ticking clocks, of times to eat and sleep; the athlete's garb for austere minutes per week; jogging bellies, pendulous chests, sagging buttocks, in a gasp for longevity. Beds, like immobility, frightened him. Without brandy there was no sleep; with it, a kind of sweaty nightmare that somehow recharged him for hours unspecified.

'Neelan,' he said to Morgan. 'Cassie turned him over.' He held up the roll of notes and pocketed them again. 'Mackessy is still holding strong.'

'Clever bastards,' Morgan said.

If there was need to talk it was spaced and desultory. Morgan remembered a con-artist with camel coat and racing-bins who was always rushing to Kempton or Brighton or some other magic playground, for just one horse, one race. Pro stuff! He'd do you a favour, lay a ten for you, if you parted. Morgan laughed. Another drink. The juggernauts were gathering now, their rumble, and their shadows on the windows as the traffic-lights spaced them out.

'You won't ever retire, Cal.'

'Hardly.'

Tomorrow would be a long haul and he wished it were morning, the first light, and the burden of sleep suffered for another spell. The red flickering bedroom.

'Cover yourself well tomorrow, Taff. A long day.'

Morgan nodded.

The mice were gathering too, sounds of them in discarded litter, in waste-bins; a tap was dripping into a copper hemisphere, old as Gladstone. Calnan thought of the pewter glittering in Morgan's daily care and microcosmic distorted worlds on the curved serried lines of tumblers. And Brennan.

'That tap,' Morgan said.

'It needs a washer.'

'I'll bring one tomorrow.'

'The mice are back.'

'Demolitions,' Morgan said. 'Leaves them without house or home, poor little bastards. They don't take to the high-rise.'

'Or people.'

The traffic came and went but somehow left behind it a wash of blue-tinged light; it impinged, made a bastard pulsing rhythm, almost a sound, that was caught and repelled by glass, mirrors, the angled planes of counter. Words vanished, even silence fell away from them. Calnan's great bulk seemed to be prised from its chair. Morgan was quick as a terrier.

'What's up?'

'Law.'

The blue lights struck and slithered across Morgan's face.

'Ari's spirits?' Calnan said.

'Christ!' Morgan said; he pointed. 'Down there. In their cases!'

'A lot of Law,' Calnan said; he nodded caution to Morgan. 'Have your drink at the counter. I'll talk.'

Outside, the corner was sealed off, three cars, three whirling blue beacons, panic-makers, flinging light at them; the pavements seemed crowded as Saturday High Street; the crash of a dozen car doors, in and out of rhythm, was thunderous.

The door bell rang: someone was leaning on it. It rang and rang. They were hammering now. On the windows too.

Calnan opened the door and was sent staggering in before

133

the thrust of shoulders tight as a scrummage. Someone spun him round, almost off balance, and the face was blurred in its closenes.

'Don't move! Not a hand, not a foot! Get it?'

Fingers like hardwood canes jabbed into Calnan's gut, sent breath running for cover.

'Right? Get it?'

Calnan was still as a pillar.

The moments of practised confusion were played like an overture: bodies against bodies and the thump of feet was a display of weaponry; orders, shouts, deployment, clockwork chaos, profanity, a table knocked, a stool, the clatter of an ashtray, a voice somewhere ordering restraint, a reminder of savagery on a fraying leash. And finally the uneven arrival of silence.

The picture cleared now, the face moved away from him. Calnan picked up his glass.

'Put it down, please.' The voice came from a figure, smaller it seemed than the rest, a voice polished, rounded, quiet, all the confidence of an army behind it.

'You're in my house,' Calnan said. 'What do you want?'

From behind, a fist like a maul struck his elbow, the brandy slapped him in the face, the glass bounced unbroken along the carpet, reached the lino surround at the counter and rocked noisily to silence.

Morgan had moved and was suddenly upped and hurried to a seat, put in care. Calnan's squinting glance was a careful message.

'Who's in charge here?' the small man asked.

He was the chief, Calnan knew, and he said very mildly. 'You are.'

The jab of iron fingers again, from behind now. 'No jokes, you thick plank. Just answers. That's all.'

'Are you the guv'nor?'

'The landlord. Yes.'

The chief was a well-educated young man, thirty perhaps,

134

thoroughly inoffensive, well dressed: an expensive suit, shirt, tie, polished black shoes: he had a Home Office warrant to search for persons involved in acts of terrorism . . . or evidence of such persons having been harboured at any time . . . to search for firearms . . . or other evidence of subversive activity . . .

Calnan looked beyond him now at the full strength of the sortie: all big frames, a couple or more gone to flesh but strong as lumbering animals, the rest honed down for battle; two in uniform and flat peaked caps faced each other across the length of the bar and held sleek chained Alsatian dogs at the ready; the rest, eight Calnan counted, were grim-faced as villains, the formality of two-piece suits draping them uneasily.

Whatever scrambling system blots out the sudden advent of shock was dissipating now and Calnan was aware of a task force facing him and a moment of chill in guts and spine that might be uncertainty. Or fear. Anger raged for a moment inside him and was held in check. For how long was anger held in check, he wondered? Whatever the cost?

One of the tall shadowy men – the lieutenant, Calnan would dub him; the rest were soldiers – arranged a table and a chair for his chief and ensconced him with strict formality; a folder came from a briefcase and was perused, occasionally squinted at, in the half-light. He nodded, he was ready: some venerable pile of masonry and learning had equipped him to lead, to delegate unpleasantness, accept its necessity.

The lieutenant called out to Calnan, 'Come here!' A distance of perhaps three paces but a great journey into serfdom, Calnan knew. 'Stand here!'

Calnan moved to his position, obeyed, saw Morgan's tortured eyes look away in search of some other anchor of vision.

Name, age, nationality, the whole laborious rigmarole was played out for Calnan and each reply was a submission.

Calnan thought of Ari, the Greek. Nationality? Where I make money.

The soldiers were summoned from the shadows, sent on their missions: floor one, floor two, basement-cellar. Half a dozen toneless words perhaps: tight-lipped silence and a kind of smouldering resentment was the mask of each role. Only the chief was kind, human. His lieutenant, a waiting Cerebus, stood at his chair; the dogs and their attendants watched; from the house came the ungentle sounds of rummaging.

Eyes on Calnan, a finger pointed at Morgan, the lieutenant said, 'What's this? A barman?'

'Manager.'

That was amusing; even the dog-men laughed.

'Manager for a Mick, Big, big job!'

The chief said, 'Are you a member of a political group, Mr Calnan?'

'No.'

'Do you have political sympathies of any kind?'

'No.'

'Do you ever think of politics?'

'No.'

The lieutenant said, 'Do you ever think?'

'For Christ's sake! . . .' Morgan started, but a dog, permitted a yard of chain, snarled him back to his seat.

'Keep your mouth shut, laddie,' he was told.

Calnan looked out at the familiar brick of the street, the packs of traffic on the loose. He heard the noise now only if he listened, and he looked away from the blue lights strobing into his consciousness: you could win some battles only by losing. He remembered the graves and the sadness of the angel, a greasy sergeant, a historian, the toughie on the steps: there, perhaps, it had all taken seed. Reasons were unimportant, or searching for them was a dangerous trait of humanity. Anger, quiet as the morning on Cassie's lake, was the thing: it was such a short obliging step to punishing mazes and cattle-trucks. Anger. Calnan hung it like a sign behind them in the dark and stared.

'What do you think of bombings, Mr Calnan?'

'Speak up!' the lieutenant said.

'You're not going to answer, Mr Calnan?'

A soldier from the upstairs search came bearing a street directory. 'In his room, sir.'

'Is this yours, Mr Calnan?'

'No.'

The chief examined folded-back pages. 'Xs, Mr Calnan. A lot of Xs. Earls Court, Holland Park, Old Bailey . . .'

Calnan was thinking – a great effort now – of the warm affection of brandy, deserted night-time streets full of ghostly life. Walking, walking . . .

'Bombs, you bastard!' the lieutenant roared at him.

The soldier had gone; another, from the cellar, had taken his place as if it were all a carefully choreographed exercise. Now it was a moment of hushed consultation and chief and subordinate retired, their footsteps hollow on the grimy stairs and then hard on the flagged cellar floor, fading.

'I could make you talk, you pile of shit,' the lieutenant said. 'Take you down for seven days and talk to you all the time.' He circled Calnan, loathing him from his shoes up. 'Talk to you like this!' He sunk his elbow like a piston into the soft kidney flesh above the hip: the pain exploded and shot to extremities. 'Seven days, you fat slime!'

Calnan looked beyond him at anger cold as the cellar flags.

'I'd make you shit windy.'

Fear was what they wanted. And anger, secret as terror, devoured it.

The chief returned. The briskness of business. He was in his seat again, his lieutenant in attendance.

'Unbroken cases of spirits, Mr Calnan? You have an invoice for them? Brewery purposes. Revenue purposes. You're not very communicative, are you?'

'No.'

'And these?'

Soldiers were arriving now with a dozen bundles of tools and site gear; they piled them in a mound about him, like kindling, as if they might burn him: donkeys, boots, floats, hammers, chisels, trowels, levels, tapes, lines, denims, dungarees, saws; all the unredeemed pledges of the past.

'Are these yours?'

'No.'

'Do you employ labour?'

'No.'

'If someone called and asked for a change of clothes, they could be handy, don't you think?'

'No.'

There was a long silence. The chief lit a cigarette, perused the sheets in his file, sometimes allowed his fingers to make a drumming galloping sound. Eventually he said, 'You're a convicted thief, Mr Calnan. Two years. Wandsworth . . . you were thirty years of age . . . entrusted to collect wage packets for work in . . . Hertfordshire . . . A van. You drove it into the pillar of a country gateway . . . protested you had been robbed.' He looked without expression or emotion at Calnan. '. . . Bad luck you were observed . . . not very clever. Two thousand, one hundred and eighty-eight pounds. Unrecovered.'

'Enough for a pub,' the lieutenant said. 'Two pubs!'

The chief considered it. 'Or to assist friends in need. Participation? There were bombs then too, Mr Calnan. Arms raids. You remember?'

The searchers had all returned; one brought notes in an untidy bundle from under Calnan's pillow, laid them on the table, rejoined the pack: they stood grouped in a background gloom, a posed melancholy old-boys' reunion caught by a passing camera.

'Are these yours?'

'Yes.'

'Check them.' Calnan would have taken them to the counter. 'Check them here where I can see you.'

He watched Calnan's powerful steady hands, the speed, the deftness.

'How much?'

Calnan told him.

'Is that correct?'

'Yes,' Morgan said from the darkness. A chain slackened a little, a dog growled.

'I told you, barman, didn't I?' the lieutenant said and waited.

'You did.'

The chief waited. 'Is that correct, Mr Calnan?'

'Yes.'

In a little while he began to read aloud, very slowly, from his papers.

'"... yard-man, navvy, sweeper, driver ... licensee." Versatile, Mr Calnan,' he said, 'aren't you?' There was a hint of bored impatience in his voice, more lethal than the lieutenant's war-dance. 'And a thief, of course.' He pointed. 'Pick up that money and put it in your pocket.'

Calnan obeyed.

'I'm going to think about you from time to time,' he said; he surveyed the scattered clothing and the litter of tools from the cellar. 'A bit of a mess, isn't it? I doubt if my men enjoyed handling it.'

He stood and turned his back to Calnan. They went: the dog-handlers, the chief, his soldiers. The lieutenant paused a moment, carefully packed the briefcase and locked it.

He said to Calnan. 'I don't like fat greasy thieves like you. I could leave you very sore for a few days. Very sore. When I come again I might even find a shooter up there. We can always find something when we want to, fat man.'

He tipped the table over so that it fell on Calnan's feet, shattered a forgotten glass. He went. In thirty seconds the pulses of blue light were gone, the little army, the dogs. Silence. The juggernauts from the traffic-lights filled their stage once more, came and went.

Calnan stood at the window for a long time, examined it all as if in an action replay, held here and there a frame, played and replayed it again and again. When he turned Morgan was looking across at him.

'You're sorry, Taff, aren't you?'

'Something like that,' Morgan said. 'But that's the wrong little word. If I could buy a drink, that might say something.'

'Buy me a brandy.'

'You see!' Morgan said; he gazed about the bar, gesturing at the empty space of it. 'It didn't happen, did it? A nod and a boozy dream, that's all.' And then he fixed on the mound of clothing and tools, walked to it, kicked a metal float and sent it skittering towards the fireplace, walked on the shards of broken glass to hear them crunching beneath his feet. 'But it did happen!'

'It happened,' Calnan said.

'It's the kind of poxed-up bad joke I don't like,' Morgan said; his anger was a rush of dangerous amusement now. 'They set off Southend illuminations outside our door, bust in with the two-legged dogs and Alsatians, tip your drink up, do the karate bit, search the house, fuck everything about, insult us like pigs, you, me, sit down, stand up, shut up! Bombs my bollicks, Cal! And that big bastard mouth says he might come back and fit you up! What's happening, Cal, what's happening for Christ's sake? They can't do that . . .!'

Morgan seemed to run short on breath, a confused harassed man. He drank his rum.

'Another drink,' Calnan said.

Morgan looked at Calnan's bulk silhouetted against the window, the glow of the gas fire barely reaching him.

Calnan said, 'They can do it. Get us a drink.'

'Bust in on a man's house with a small army in the middle of the night!'

'They can do it.'

Morgan went and brought the drinks. When he was calm

140

and in charge again he said, 'A mob like that could terrorise the manor, the whole country.'

'They're preventing terrorism,' Calnan said.

The pay-telephone rang and he answered. It was Cassie from across the way.

'Are you all right, Cal?'

'Fine.'

'You got the full treatment, dogs and all, mate!'

'The best.'

'I'll come and have an orange juice tomorrow.'

'Do that.'

Morgan walked about, picked up the metal float and put it with the pile, looked at the broken glass, the wet stain on Calnan's shirt, and remembered his own indignities.

'Why?' he asked Calnan.

'Out there on the pavements a man got a midge in his eye one summer,' Calnan said. 'I hooked it out with spit and a handkerchief and all that bothered him was how a smut with a world of space for aerobatics should perch on his eyeball.'

Morgan's humour was returning.

'They didn't come for bombs and desperadoes. Or even bent booze,' Calnan said. 'They came with the frighteners, that's all.'

'Frightened?' Morgan asked.

'Uneasy,' Calnan said eventually.

'They could have had your bankroll.'

'Might be better if they had. I'm going to sit here and sleep for a couple of hours. If I can.'

'Your gear's ready . . . white shirt, all that. Up there.' Morgan said. 'If the crazy gang haven't pitched them about . . .' He looked at his watch. 'I'll see you soon, won't I?'

'I was thirty when I pinched the payroll, Taff,' Calnan said. 'A good age. I knew where to put it.'

'You did a very fair job,' Morgan said, looking about. He nodded at the floor. 'Bleedin' breaker's yard, eh? Brennan'll strain his nuts on that lot!'

141

The door clicked shut and Calnan could hear the sharp hammer of Morgan's heels until distance and traffic finally absorbed them.

10

It was reaching down for four-thirty when Calnan awoke; since Morgan's departure there had been, from time to time, seconds of wakefulness, an awareness of heat and fire-glow, the passing noise, the tremble of a window, and then a free fall into oblivion again. Sleep was imprisonment and escapes. He sweated in sleep, but now only a little; tensions came and went like tides and this was the neap. He was grateful. He would drink of course: a measured pace in the long calm of ebb.

He stood and saw the debris of tools and soiled clothing making a ring where he had stood, the upturned table, the glitter of broken glass. There was bruised soreness at his side and in his gut where the vicious bastard had rammed elbow and fingers. He looked at the carpet where he had taken three paces in surrender and felt more sadness than anger.

You are a convicted thief, Mr Calnan.

He went inside the counter and drank a pint tumbler of water and then a measure of brandy. This was a special day, Duffy's last trip of course, but the end too of some allotted span of activity. Whatever of this terminal morning and day-in-day-out custom that lay dissolved, dormant, in Calnan's consciousness, suddenly took shape, materialised again: a moment ago it had been the bar, now it was each fragment and colour and shape and shade that made the bar. He looked at a piece of brass trim that he had fixed on a counter flap twenty years before, the glacial attrition; even the screw heads were worn. He rubbed his hand along the years of it. The furniture was old, soiled, even ugly; here and there the carpet down to a hesian threadbareness; the ceiling, the lights, the window frames, the grained wainscoting, the doors, the worn bolts, the sandstone step, all now obtruded and seemed to distance him. It was a strange place; his time there had been allotted and spent. Illness had never laid him low but he thought that emerging after weeks, months of beds and chairs and walking-frames, sick glittering eyes would see dust, a pebble even, in the gutter, wonder at the ugliness of a bus-stop, glance at a fallen leaf trapped in a crevice. The intensity of beginnings and ends.

He paced the perimeter of the bar, touching it here and there, took brandy with him and descended the neglected worn treads to the cellar. The deep grey flagstones never dried, a thousand cobwebs joined rafter to rafter six inches above his head; and where twelve-by-twelve beams took the load he crouched to pass under. There was a dull ache in his side and his stomach stiffening, even down to his groin.

I could make you talk ... you pile of shit ... you fat slime. He remembered.

In the cellar there had been oak barrels and stillions and taps and spiles and mallets and pages once; now, white metal canisters, pipes and gas cylinders, cooling machines sprouting tubes like some forgotten turbine of dialysis.

The cellar stocks were neat and ordered as Morgan's pristine servery and all about them the rubble of years: the broken, the obsolete, the unmanageable that Brennan had contributed to: sacking, sodden carpet, maimed furniture, everything from corks to rotting woodwork.

Calnan surveyed it, wondered why he had come down to the wet chill. He drank a little. Everything was sharp and defined for his inspection. In the far corners damp fungus like candy-floss whiskered the stone and flaking limewash. Calnan had no shudders or disquiet in deserted places but, on what seemed an aimless journey, he felt somehow accompanied; he felt no uneasiness, only a certainty that, like the Clincher in his Chapels of Rest, he was not alone. Cellars – almost unchanged from generation to generation while bars and even living-space were coloured and tarted – were not only the heart and pump of the ageing body but its guts and bowels and kidneys too: beer coursed up its tubes into sparkling glasses and thick-smelling waste rattled in cast-iron downpipes and choking gullies; and every empty keg could be filled with steaming waste from the toilets. Beneath him the network of drains converged, added a spoonful to a torrent rushing down to the great tireless River.

Brewery surveyors used to make, in less frenetic times, social calls to spend an hour or so of their unmeasured days noting a blemish or two but above all to talk. It seemed a long time since people had spent unhurried days.

'Cellars are haunted,' a surveyor had once told Calnan. 'Publicans leave pieces of themselves in cellars and keep coming back for them.' He was laughing of course. He was a tall smiling figure who had been a fighting airman for king and country; and found peace and rescued commerce not only dull but sadly shop-soiled. He liked Calnan, the sudden out-rageous boom of laughter.

'Ailing publicans,' he said, 'escape to their cellars. They sit, drain their precious flasks, find peace, listen to the shuffling feet above them.'

'A kind of early grave,' Calnan said.

'Peace, Calnan.'

Calnan had shown him loose masonry where behind the stonework two yellowed stumps of bone protruded like gross blind creatures born in darkness.

'Plague bones,' he had said. 'We demolish old piles and there they are, hundreds of them. Plague pits, you know. A couple of miles of grassy fields from the City to here, once. Dig a hole out there, haul cadavers out by the cartload.'

'A lot of ghosts,' Calnan had said.

'Friendly ghosts.'

That was perhaps ten years past, Calnan thought, when they had stood here on the wet flags. He was gone now, redundant, found wanting by some latter day Kubla Khan weary of pleasure domes and Abyssinian maids.

Calnan moved towards the bones and loose masonry again. There had been a laystall beneath his feet too, a great field of it: behind the locked doors of the plagued City human waste accumulated, was pitched from split-second opened windows, a great stinking viscous quagmire of it: cartloads came endlessly from Shoreditch and Bishopsgate and flowed over the green grass. Backyard flowers here and there, a tree, had a rich table beneath them. Calnan lifted away the loose stonework and touched the bones again. He spent a long time carefully freeing them and brought them to the bar.

A drink. He felt better today: he tasted the brandy and paused in its warmth for a few moments. The bones were yellow-brown, discoloured, not full-grown, he thought: the leg bones of a growing child that had perhaps run past the houses on London Bridge or skated on the River. He wrapped them with a kind of gentle respect in dust-cloth from the cellar debris on his carpet, found cardboard and paper and sealing tape. It was a small parcel. He enclosed a note: 'Give these plague bones decent burial' and addressed it to the 'Caretaker, Leytonstone Cemetery'. He put a lot of stamps on it and went upstairs to his bedroom.

It was in darkness. He hadn't opened back the window curtains for years and when he did the dust enveloped him and the street light poured in like grey icy water. The marauding soldiers had upended his bed, left the wardrobe's contents where they fell; the dead blacked-out fire was supine before the grate and even the spare bulbs had been trampled on and shattered.

He worked at it until he had restored a bearable day-to-day untidiness but, robbed of shadows and red glow, it was desolate, without comfort. The room had died. He put the suit, shirt, handkerchief, socks, black tie, that Morgan had arranged, on the bed: but for dust smears they had survived the ballywrack.

He drank again and smoothed and stacked his bar-takings and put them in the safe. He laid the wrapped bones beside them and turned the key. He felt happier: behind the disorder of every day there was always a regimen that he imposed upon himself, a discipline that embraced shopkeeping and drinking or whatever eructions a day's trade might bring. Now it was a time of change and he would have to meet it: the sharp edges of everything in his bar, the street lights invading his red room, the memories of things in the cellar, were a fade-out, the end of a scene. But he remembered the chief, and the disparagement, bled of even the merest trace of emotion, left unease. There had to be even crude rules for a fair fight. There were no rules.

You are a convicted thief, Mr Calnan . . .

The decision to steal had been made in an instant. He had driven in through Barnet and Whetstone and Finchley, where the office was, and signed for a small brown-papered parcel. Seven hundred and twenty-eight pounds. Twenty fives was a hundred: a parcel small enough to sit deep in a donkey pocket. Walking the corridors to the lift he had tried to count the heads behind desks and tables in the boundless spaces beyond glass walls. Two hundred, perhaps more: faces intent, blank, restless; wrist-watches ticking. But how young they were, it struck him. And he was thirty, it was his birthday. An office door inscribed 'Manager' was partly open and a stylish man in cream cuff-linked shirt and silken tie, smoked, laughed, talked to a telephone. Calnan had stopped an instant to ponder it all but he saw the angry wave of the cuff-link and the door had been shut like a hammer-blow. And the face had been young.

That was the moment. He had a room in Dalston and he had driven there, counted his pounds, seven hundred and twenty-eight, made the parcel neater; even dumped silver and copper, tied in grease-wiper, deep in the refuse bin of a transport caff before he pushed on to the Trade Winds.

It had been lunchtime and the guv'nor said, 'No school today, Pat?'

'Passing through. Time for a pint,' Calnan told him.

'One pint of best coming up, Pat, me boy,' he said, sing-song, practised as a bingo-caller.

After more than six years it was still 'Pat' and 'Pat, me boy'. But he belonged. A few years and it would be 'Old Pat'. Old Pat was in last night . . .

Calnan remembered the savage intensity of that day and could smile a little at it now. Every failed or prosperous face was a spur, every day of fourteen years on the trot an offence committed against him: ankle-deep in muck trenches, carving out cubes of clay heavy enough to drag at stomach and groin and leave a pale streak of weariness on cheek-bones at the end of a day; the spleen of ganger-men, the filth of rooms shared, discarded rotting clothes in corners; drink and weekend whores stripping and effing; another week, another site; the merciless fights of pickhandle and boot. And then it had been fourteen years since he had walked young from the Arch, the flagged platforms of old Euston, past the War Memorial, to look first time at the early traffic moving to King's Cross and St Pancras. Fourteen years: a room he didn't share anymore, books for a night class, a change of clothes, less than two hundred in a bank-book and he was thirty . . .

'Christ, fourteen years,' he had said, almost aloud.

'You calling, Pat?' Cliffie, the guv'nor was coming, hand raised.

'My birthday. Have a drink.'

'Half a pint with you. Pat. Twenty-one again, are we?'

'Thirty.'

'Pushing on, me boy! Forty, fifty, sixty! . . .'

Laughter; Cliffie, hard as a nut, gold watch, jewellery, flat oiled hair, centre parting, his young picture on the wall, crouched in boxing pose. He had looked expertly at Calnan's big frame, the cracked, calloused hands, a trace of weariness. 'Winter on the outside's no cop, eh?' he was saying. 'And it pisses in summer too, don't it? I'd a stall over in Ridley once. Fruit and veg. Ten year, near enough. It was good to get out of the cold . . . fucking good . . .'

Calnan had said, 'I might be out of town, the weekend. Or longer. Do me a favour.'

'If I can.'

He had laid the small wrapped package on the counter.

'Hold it for you?'

'I'd be obliged.'

'That's all right, Pat.'

He had finished his drink and as he was leaving Cliffie called out, 'No sweat, Pat. Be here when you come.' He had nodded to Calnan and smiled: 'Whenever you come.'

Old dog for the hard road; he knew the score, Calnan had thought. Whenever you come . . .

The juggernauts and roaring gears returned but the room without its glow and warmth was a strange world for a moment. He looked at his funeral clothes on the bed and the bomb-struck bathroom and went downstairs again to the bar. The gnawing restlessness needed a drink but he thought of the long day and postponed it. It was strange to remember Euston at sixteen: and almost a quarter of a century had passed since he had stood here at the counter pushing the loot across to Cliffie. He looked at the door where he had stood and Cliffie was calling out, 'Whenever you come, Pat.'

He had pulled into a public jakes in Finsbury Park, pushed the empty wage envelopes with his hand around the bend of the toilet-pan, flushed it twice. And then on through Finchley and out of Barnet towards Potter's Bar. It was a perishing wind coming across the bare acres of tillage-land, shaking the winter hedges. There was his iron gateway, the heavy stone pillars and, in the charcoaled distance, a half-mile perhaps, a red smudge of telephone booth. He had waited for an empty road in his mirror and charged at the pillar, standing on the brake and hitting it on the skid.. He had walked to and from the telephone and awaited the Law . . .

'And so they pushed you off the road now, Paddy bejasus, and took your money?'

'That's right.'

'And no one saw them?'

'That's right.'

'And they were up and gone and you never got a number? You were confused.'

'That's right.'

'And there was the telephone?'

'That's right.'

'And you don't know how much. Six, seven hundred, maybe.'

'That's right.'

He remembered they had backed him against the iron gate, stood smiling for a long time.

'What's half six hundred, Pat?'

'Three.'

'That's right! A real bargain. We wouldn't want to knock you playing stock-cars with a gatepost, would we now? . . . Upset his worship no end . . .'

But he had sat it out: a month in the somnolence of Brixton, the dock for thirty minutes, two years in the cleansing sink of Wandsworth. There had been a litany of resisting arrest, abuse, violence, damage to vehicle, to property . . . and there had been more than two thousand in the wage packets, he had been told . . .

Everyone should tangle with the Law, take the stand, do a little time. A novitiate. He had read for two years, watching his hands become soft and human: prison was the stench of slopping out, sex-battles, boredom, hold your corner, pitiless eyes for everything: he would always remember the sounds of it, day and night.

He thought about Cliffie standing there that lunchtime: gold rings, gold watch, gold tie-pin, rich nourishment shining on his hard face, eyes glittering with life.

In two years the eyes were dying. Calnan had come up

from Wandsworth and found him, still in humour, but wasting.

'You did a bit, Pat?' he had said.

'Two.'

'It passes.' He brought Calnan's package of money. 'Not a bad little house, this. Out of the cold. It's cold out there . . .'

Calnan climbed to the flat roof and watched the light creeping in again from beyond the last fringes of the East End. Cliffie was buried out in Manor Park where weeds grew four foot high. He supposed he too had walked the cellar and bar and rooms for a last time.

Calnan remembered the chief and his lieutenant with quite distant anger. The sound of a train with a huge ribbed container of some lethal waste came up the line from Highbury: youth sometimes waved banners there and aimed their cameras. It didn't matter a lot to the ageing. The trains were relentless. Calnan wondered how he would be lessened, parcelled up like old bones, ousted. It was an end. The light was coming in across the strange beauty of buildings, haphazard shapes spilt from a sack, and he was feeling at ease, ready for it.

Brennan arrived after seven, resplendent as a pallbearer, anxious a moment and then smiling to hide overweening curiosity. He off-loaded first.

'There won't be sandwiches . . .'

'Forget it.'

'Yes, yes. I came dressed for the funeral, Cal,' he said. 'Save a journey home and back.'

'Careful you don't pick up any dirt,' Calnan said.

Brennan was looking at the vast debris thrown up by the night. 'What is it?' he asked.

'Money,' Calnan told him. 'Get a spieler from the market with a van. He'll take it and pay you.'

'Mine?'

Calnan nodded.

'What can I say, Cal? I can use a few bob at a time like this.'

'There's dungarees there, rubber boots, a cap. Put them on.'

Brennan gazed in uncertainty.

'There's cleaning and a day's work to be done here. And down there.' Calnan pointed to the cellar. 'You look like a puff sailing home from a party. Cover yourself.'

Brennan almost smiled to be suddenly in the familiar rough and tumble of another day. When he had togged and donned the cap he felt pleased. 'When you look at it, it's the sensible thing,' he said. 'I should get myself a rig. It wouldn't cost a fortune and there'd be fair wear in it.'

'Last you a lifetime.' Calnan was at the window. 'Why don't you keep that lot?'

'Second-hand gear? I was never keen on it. Everything has a history. It could be dirt, disease, even a bad wish left on it when times were rocky.'

'Times are always rocky for someone.'

'Second-hand is dodgy, Cal.'

'Except watches.'

Brennan said suddenly, 'I'll make a phone call. I know a client with a van. I can't put a sparkle on the place until the floor is clear.'

Calnan watched a milk-float groaning, clinking past. There had been a whole strike-force of them once and a depot big as a stadium up the road: four o'clock, the first crash of crate stacks at the loading bank, and at five a whining rattling diaspora in motion. Good drinkers too: a bar full of them at lunchtime. A handful left now. The chain stores and the Pakis sold paper cartons; and bottles on doorsteps had a kind of out of tune ingenuous honesty.

Brennan was coming back from the phone. 'He's on his way. He does a bit of totting. Always on the move. No great rush on building gear, he said. But he'll do me a favour.'

'You believed him?'

'He's a straight man, Cal. Good as gold.'

Brennan began his sweeping at the farthest end of the bar. He liked a coarse broom that scutched before it all things dropped or discarded but left dirt behind. In the morning light he moved in a cloud of dust like a dying desert whirlwind. When he had drawn closer he said, 'I never cared for that Yorkie on the news-stand, Cal.'

'Let him be,' Calnan said. 'He's the last of the English hucksters. Bonaparte wouldn't know the place.' Brennan, he knew, had heard whisperings and he would feint and prod for confirmation. A game had to be played.

'He rabbits too much. A mouth like a bucket. If ever you hear a wild story going about you'll know it started with Yorkie.'

'I will,' Calnan said.

That halted him for a while but he warmed again. 'There comes a time when the line must be drawn. Half-door gossip is one thing but ...' he paused before unsavouriness '... character assassination is a horse of a different colour.'

'It is.'

Brennan approached and leant on his brush: rubber boots, dungarees, flat cap, he was the archetypal Mick beloved of his inferiors. 'You should be deported, Cal, that's what he said! Sent back where you belong! You're in with the bloody murdering terrorists! That's what he said and a half-dozen jossers with their ears cocked!'

'What did you say?' Calnan asked.

'What could I say?'

'That I make the bombs and you do the watches.'

'Jesus!' Brennan said, but in prayer. 'Don't joke about it! There was ten squad cars, an army of men, every dog in London, the fire brigade, the salvage, the ambulance! That's the story that's out!' Reality suddenly flared. 'Watches, watches! ... Oh my God! ... watches!'

'I was raided,' Calnan said soberly. 'Guns, bombs, men on the run? They had a file on us. Watches too. A lot of watches make their way to the Trade Winds, it seems.'

'What will I do?'

'Work.'

Calnan saw Cassie crossing the road with a swing of the hip and the hair; a juggernaut jockey hooted her and she gave him a fingers. Calnan opened the door.

'Come for a drive,' she said. 'I need company.'

'I doubt it,' Calnan said, 'but I'll come.' He said to Brennan, 'How much will he give on the gear?'

'A couple, no more.'

'When he has it on the van tell him I said, ten notes. Or I'll come and collect it. And no customers till Morgan is in there on the bridge.'

Brennan nodded.

It was seven-thirty, traffic beginning to buzz a little but still space for Cassie to push on without effort.

'My old pop was a rogue,' she said suddenly. 'A star turn. Not a villain, mind. A rogue. Whenever there was a big one they'd knock him up. He didn't mind, gave the yes–yes–yes and the no–no–no, looked upset when they disturbed the place. Casablanca, he called it: round up the usual suspects. That's the Old Bill, of course. You had the professionals. Bash the bombers. Pick a Paddy pub. Someone mightn't like you, Cal, though I can't believe that!'

She sent amusement like little tinkling bells about the car. 'Big rogues go for business, Cal,' she said, 'Pay the tax chaps, vote law and order, tut-tut the riots in Brixton.'

Calnan smiled.

'Dozens, dozens of business men in the manors round here. Nice quiet business men. A spare pad in Brighton, maybe. Maybe even one in Juan le Pins. Marbella's crowded now, scruffy. The good life, but quiet, respectable. Not cheap thieves like in the City, all the flimflam and taradiddle. Shit. Pissarse financiers! Nothing like that.'

They had jinked down through old Hackney and Victoria Park to the hinterland of Roman Road market. 'I got two shops in the market,' she said. 'Good stuff, *haute couture*, you

154

ring the bell to get in. That kind of touch. An' half a little spinner in Covent Garden too. Very posh there now.'

Calnan drank a nip or two. The street was quiet; steps rising to good honest houses that, before two world wars, wouldn't have offended a clerk. The East End had a dignity all its own.

'You don't have to bother with old dribblers on West Hill or across the Heath,' Calnan said suddenly.

'I used to have ten. Down to four now. Work out the seam, Cal, that's all.' She was laughing again. 'At fifty nicker a week times ten it wasn't a bad earner. Five years. Add it up.'

'I don't need to.'

She had stopped before the walled overgrown grounds of a rectory: iron gates, a little drive and steps to a porticoed door.

'An' never a hand on me, Cal. Sometimes a little strip-strip-hooray if I thought they mightn't topple over, like. There was a general, very strict, one leg, liked me with a Sam Browne and wellies. Stand aaat . . . ease! Keen on drill.'

Calnan was smiling.

'This way,' she said.

She unlocked the gateway and door. It was a two- and three-storied house of beauty and substance, sitting among old elms on a couple, perhaps three, acres with its twin coach-house and stables and encircling drive. The church that had faced it across the way wasn't even a memory: a block of private flats sat there now: shrubs, a garden, garages: tasteful.

'A friend of mine,' she said.

'Business.'

'Big man.'

The Rectory was Cassie's. She was restoring it, she said. A few changes: lighting, bathrooms, that was all. She liked old houses.

'It's costing a bit but it's going to be special.'

And she liked to get there before the workmen: keep the score, watch for strokes.

155

Calnan nodded.

They walked the corridors and stairs and the huge spacious rooms. It would be a club: a hundred members, no more, at a monkey a time: snooker, sauna, punters' lounge, big-screen telly, phones, phones, phones; gym and tone up, sit an' talk room, no wives, no birds, and what's a home without a bar; some shrubs and flowers out there but mostly car space. Every member has his key. Special . . .

In the car Calnan said, 'A fine place.'

'You like it?'

'Yes.'

'Well, Cal,' she said, 'with the fuzz behind you an' a funeral up front, I thought a morning drive might cheer you up.'

'Right.'

'I'll come and have a juice some time today. With the mourners.'

She dropped him on the High Road and sped away before the tightening grip of morning peak.

Calnan walked to the florists and little Joe Koski, in his cap, said, 'Glad you came, Cal. A lot of news about. Glad to see you. Someone tried to cancel. I was worried.'

'A Gates of Heaven?' Calnan asked.

'That's it there. Monster size. Biggest I do. I said I was worried, didn't I?'

'You did. I want a wreath too. Special. And on the card: *I am beside you – Elmer Devine*. If anybody asks, it was a telephone job, American accent, and the money, all of it, plain envelope, came in dollars.'

Koski was motionless in the assimilation of everything. 'Very late for a wreath, Cal,' he felt obliged to say.

'Just do it. How much? And don't get greedy, Joe. This morning I feel poverty-stricken. The Gates of Heaven, the lot. How much?'

Calnan paid him. 'All in dollars, remember?' He pushed on to Ari's.

156

The warm smell of weekday breakfast-time waited at the door, blurred the windows. The room was filling.

Ari came and said. 'All right, Cal?' He was anxious.

Calnan nodded. 'They weren't looking for booze.'

'I hear everything, Cal!' Ari might be laughing or snarling. 'Christ, Cal, bloody bombs! It's too much . . . too much!'

'Do they die in Cyprus?' Calnan asked.

'When they can't help it.'

'And people have food and a piss-up?'

Ari smiled. 'OK, Cal! I do the food for you. Myself!'

'Half-past four.'

'Now you want breakfast.'

157

11

When the wind blew in from the East End it filled the streets with sudden gusts, a stinging wind. It had risen while Calnan was at Ari's: it watered the eyes, hunched the shoulders. He turned away from the High Road towards the Trade Winds and it followed him. But he was impervious behind his flesh and Ari's food.

Passing the sex shop he knew the Polack was at the window, peering from the cover of apparatus and lingerie, and with a coin he double-rapped on the glass – a splintering sound – and called out, 'Caught you, you bastard!' There was noise but the wind carried it off: he hoped the Polack was arse over tip in his rutting machines.

Wang, at the Chinese takeaway, was filled with compassion. In the gusts of wind he might be weeping. 'Mr Trade Winds! Mr Trade Winds!' He stood on the pavement, hands outstretched, a crucifix, words airy as ectoplasm formed down in some throaty compartment and barely reached his lips. Calnan wondered at the miracle of speech.

'You pay, Mr Trade Winds! . . . Hong Kong everyone pay . . . pay . . . pay!'

One hand held a knife, the other a clump of pale greenery.

'You're next, Wang,' Calnan said. 'Prawn balls, cannon-balls, bean-shoots, dynamite.'

He moved on. Morgan was in his servery; Brennan, in protective clothing, a false picture of diligence. And, at the

158

counter, Neelan and Mackessy in conspiracy. They looked at him for gaping wounds of the early morning débâcle.

Mackessy shook his head in sorrow. 'What can I say, Cal?'

They were starting on brandy again.

'Nothing,' Calnan said.

'SB, I suppose?' Neelan asked expertly and in the silence nodded his own affirmative. 'I thought so. Lucky we weren't here. They might have had us on sus.'

Morgan laughed: he bit on a huge red apple and the sound was like crackling wood.

Brennan sucked his teeth. 'Strange, I never had any desire for fruit,' he said. 'Even the sound of it, like that, puts my teeth on edge. Bananas I can stand. If you pushed me I might take a banana.'

'Try not to worry about it,' Calnan said; the tools and gear were gone and but for the smashed mirrors of wall and cabinet the neglect might have escaped scrutiny: the floors had an illusion of cleanliness; but Morgan's glistening island was a high altar.

'What did the rag-and-bone man give you?'

'He's a dealer, Cal.'

'What did he give you?'

'Seven,' Brennan said eventually.

'That's about right.'

'You said ten.'

'I know.'

Neelan had got down from his stool: black and yellow discolouration sat on his cheek-bone; he patted his groin and looked bravely ahead. 'There are a few matters for discussion this morning, Cal, wouldn't you say?'

Calnan ignored him. He said to Morgan, 'I'll wash and change.' It was pushing for ten o'clock. 'There'll be early mourners for sure.' He moved off to his private door and, midway on the stairs, took a mouthful of brandy.

He could hear Neelan: 'Ignorant bollicks! He could ask a man how he felt, couldn't he? A few lousy pounds. I'm sorry

I raised my hand to defend it!'

'There's no smoke without fire,' Mackessy said obliquely.

Brennan said, 'You mean bombs?'

'What else?'

'The Law doesn't spend time and money flying round like farts in a thunderstorm. Dogs, fire brigades, a battalion of manpower!' Neelan said and made a great punctuation of pause. 'And every innocent man that steps through that door today is being watched. Keep that in mind.'

'I'll bet he changed his tune for the Law,' Mackessy said. '"Good evening, gentlemen, and can I get you something?" All smiles and salutes. A pity they didn't lean on him.'

'Lean!' Neelan's laugh was a cackle. 'All that belly and wind! A fast jab and he's on his back like a beetle.'

'God forbid. There's enough violence,' Brennan said.

'What did you sell for him?' Neelan asked, quick as a flash.

'Scrap from the cellar.'

'Tools?' Mackessy said.

'If you could call them that.'

'Seven quid?'

'I left it upstairs for him,' Brennan said. 'That man wouldn't give his steam to the john.'

There was silence; only Morgan's movements behind the counter disturbed it. Neelan said eventually, 'Seven quid for a pile of rubbish! A decent man would have put it in your fist and told you to raise your glass to Jim Duffy. A mean man is a terrible thing.'

Calnan waited for the next rumble of traffic and climbed to his landing. When he had washed and shaved and donned his change of clothes and drunk a measure of brandy he came down noisily, giving warning of his arrival.

'You look like a man from the City,' Mackessy said with a great show of admiration.

'A stockbroker, at least. If not chief cashier at the Bank of England,' Neelan said. 'We were wondering about the kitty.'

'The kitty. The beer money,' Mackessy explained, apologised.

Neelan smiled at the pettiness of things. 'The few quid you owe us for the upstairs job. A ton, wasn't it? From now on people will arrive and it doesn't look good to hold out an empty hand.'

'Subscribers will be arriving,' Calnan amended it. 'You could pin up that list for a start.'

Neelan stared at him, thunderstruck. 'The list, Cal, was stolen with the money! Surely you understood that! Whoever has the money has the list! That's the end of it!' He drank his brandy and clapped his glass on the counter, bellicose, very confident now. 'They like to see their names on the wall, all that vanity crap, we know that. And who gave what and how much did we raise? But hard lines for a gold watch! They'll have to grin and bear it. I'm the one that stood my ground, took the boot in defence of their miserable pence and ha'pence!'

Mackessy took his place beside him and said to Calnan. 'And when you put a ton in the kitty, that'll be our ton! Out of here!' He tapped his pocket. 'We can't do better than that.'

'No,' Calnan agreed; he looked from one to the other. 'Who's making the speech?'

'Speech?'

'You must get credit for pushing out a ton. A fair sum. And you could mention about broken dreams and all that, of course.' Calnan looked at their poker-masks and wondered at the magnificent computers whirring behind them. 'The seat in the park, trees and shrubs, Jim Duffy up to his arse in flowers.'

'You're gone over the top now,' Neelan said with outrageous cheek. 'A man doesn't want credit for that kind of thing. The less said the better.'

'Exactly,' Mackessy said. 'Short and sweet.' He summoned Morgan. 'Pencil and paper like a good man. Something like, "Following the robbery of the J. Duffy collection last night,

Mr Neelan and Mr Mackessy personally contribute the sum of one hundred pounds to provide a farewell occasion for his friends. Thank you." '

'Grand!' Neelan smiled. 'My hand is a bit stiff but I'll manage to print it.'

'"The Duffy Collection",' Morgan said. 'Sounds like a bust-up at the National Gallery. What about the food?'

'Brennan's department.' Neelan waved it away, already poised for calligraphy.

'Food?' Brennan said. 'I explained to the guv'nor. There'll be no food.'

They stared at him.

'The missus won't budge.'

'For a dead man's send-off! God forgive her and her brood.' Mackessy paced about, head shaking.

'Looks mean but we'll make the best of it.' Neelan aimed at Calnan, raised his glass, returned stoically to his artwork.

'Yes,' Mackessy said with fresh resolve. 'Put up the kitty, Cal, and we'll be ready for our guests.'

'The kitty goes up after the funeral,' Morgan said with a dangerous grin. 'The punters pay their way till then.'

Calnan nodded philosophically. 'The custom,' he said.

Mackessy laughed. 'A man can't handle his own money, is that it?'

Neelan, strangely, was the peacemaker. 'Two brandies,' he said with great emphasis. 'Large brandies.' He put a ten on the counter and said to Calnan, 'I raised a few flags against the exhibition work this morning.'

'You could have put it in the kitty,' Morgan said.

'And sponge all day? You're not in the valleys now, boyo!'

Brennan had raced across the skimpy catalogue of his labours, discarded his clobber and swanned about in sanctimonious dignity that would have delighted the Clincher. In this time, before official opening, he answered door bells and ushered in smiling, surprised, decently suited men: for them funerals were not items to be slotted in a day's schedule: a funeral took time, and schedules like mourners fell in behind it. Instinctively they found the remote corners of the bar, furthest from windows and peeping light. Brennan was moving among them offering the night's events – the mug, the dip, dogs and bomb-boys, wounds – in small pieces, in hushed confidence. He accepted drinks only with reluctance.

Calnan watched, acknowledged nods and the raised glasses of solidarity. There was no escape. He thought of the rolling tide of spurious fame and hyperbole that would soon be breaking on a thousand shores; and the clever cowardice of submission it took to survive.

Neelan clicked his fingers, with a weary smile summoned Brennan from down the bar: the curlicued notice was posted and its seed broadcast from head to head: glasses were raised again, a profusion of drinks sent to the men of courage and generosity. Well done! Well done! Neelan went to walk among them, deprecating excesses of emotion and even mild applause; he tilted his discoloured face to the light, pointed modestly at his groin and limped a little.

Mackessy, out of joint, eventually recalled him. 'Enough is enough,' he said. 'We don't want to get lumbered in rounds of drink as long as your arm.'

'In the circumstances I'm expected to mix a little,' Neelan said. 'That's all. Drinks?' and he gestured at perhaps a dozen waiting brandies Morgan had served. 'Gifts. Marks of appreciation. My visit just a way of saying, thank you.'

'Christ!' Calnan said, almost aloud.

Morgan was grinning wickedly as he went about his chores.

Brennan, drinks consumed, drink in hand, returned. 'Decent men,' he said.

'I don't want them taken advantage of,' Neelan told him. 'So, close down, Brennan, and stick with glasses and ashtrays. If there's talking to be done, I'll do it.'

Mackessy, carefully excluded, lessened, demeaned, was glinting with anger. He held up his glass and boomed, 'Thank you, gentlemen. Your health and wealth!'

163

Again, raised glasses, responses filling the air.

'Just a little thank you,' he said to Neelan.

The doorbell rang and Calnan saw the outline of Koski's van through the window. Brennan, head bowed, held open the door and the flowers were carried in, displayed prominently on a couple of tables pulled together where light fell on them. Calnan watched the tightening of Neelan's fist, the alarm signal to Mackessy. The Gates of Heaven was a wire frame, close-plaited with flowers and foliage, its gates opening in welcome for Duffy. But Calnan's wreath was the showstopper, more dignified, prestigious. And it had mystery. They watched in restiveness while Koski's man placed and arranged. Now, bill in hand, he would come smiling for his money and they braced themselves. No deal, order cancelled. Attack, outrage, would be the battle order. They were ready. But he respectfully left a receipted invoice and was gone. Brennan, unsteady, dirty-pale as a dying lily, came to them from the flowers. They were recovering like veterans.

'Who sent the wreath?' Neelan asked.

Brennan snatched a brandy at random and drank it back; he scanned the bar with an instant beam of fear.

Mackessy was outraged. With the stealth of a bird man he gripped the seat of Brennan's pants and lifted him until Brennan was on the threshold of a screech. He released him. 'That'll cost you a brandy, Flip-flop. Tap on the counter.'

'Who sent the wreath, I asked you?' Neelan said again, already pointing his admiration towards Calnan.

Brennan gazed at them; and at Calnan. 'The wreath,' he said, 'is from Elmer Devine.'

'Who?' Calnan said.

'Elmer Devine.'

Calnan looked with what might be a trace of confusion, annoyance, at the flowers, and slowly peered from face to face around the bar. He turned to inspect the walls and vacant chairs behind him. 'That Clincher is a funny character,' he said.

'Why?' Neelan asked.

Mackessy drank.

'He could feel the presence,' Brennan said. 'The presence of Elmer Devine.'

'Balls!' Neelan said; he walked to the wreath and back, stood in silence, drank a brandy, sipped another.

'Elmer Devine?' Mackessy asked.

Neelan didn't answer: he took the invoice to the pay-phone and rang Koski's number. He came back with uncertainty showing. 'There's a joker in the deck somewhere,' he said.

'Well?' Mackessy said.

'Elmer Devine?' Calnan asked.

Neelan was sullen now, still in conflict. 'Plain envelope in the box this morning, no stamp, no letter. Dollars. And the phone rings.'

'American accent?' Calnan said.

'That's right. Elmer Devine.'

Calnan nodded and Morgan brought a large brandy. He ignored them, seemed deep in thought. The doorbell rang again and Brennan stood in a sweat of apprehension.

'Open it,' Calnan told him.

It was Morgan's staff, Blondie and Sher; brilliant, vibrant, creamed, coiffured, prancing to their work, putting death to shame.

They said to Neelan:

'You look like a corpse, hunky.'

'Yeah, week old.'

Neelan looked at their legs and bums and could feel no passion. He divided the remaining brandies between Mackessy and himself.

Brennan called for beer and his hand trembled a little, beer flopped on the counter.

'Christ!' Mackessy said. 'Don't wet yourself!'

Calnan went slowly to inspect the flowers and returned and drank and pondered in silence for a long time. 'When the

Law took off last night,' he said, 'I sat there and slept for ten minutes. I awoke, and every door in the house was banging and the wind was perishing. Cold, like I never felt before. I get to the bottom of the stairs and there isn't a sound. And upstairs, every door and window shut and silent. Silent as a tomb. Not even a sound of traffic or the creak of a floorboard. It was like standing in a strange house.' He looked from face to face, eyes to eyes. 'And when I came back and sat here it started up again.'

'God between us and all harm!' Brennan drank noisily and remembered to cross himself.

'And then, like the Clincher,' Calnan said, 'I knew someone had arrived.'

'A presence?' Brennan whispered.

'There was great peace. I slept a couple of hours.'

'Elmer Devine?'

Calnan drank and considered it. 'Who am I to say?' He turned to Neelan. 'Were all the flowers paid for?'

Neelan shrugged the unimportance of it. 'All of them, I suppose,' he said.

'Just as well or we might have had Joe Koski hammering on the door for the Gates of Heaven.'

'I could handle Joe Koski.'

'For that matter,' Mackessy said, 'Duffy couldn't stand the sight of flowers. A waste of money.'

A great surge of defensive anger was rising now; Brennan distanced himself a pace, dissociated himself.

'What about the trees and the seat in the park and every plant in Europe smothering him like weeds?' Calnan said.

'I'm tired of the whole thing!' Mackessy announced.

'The same as that!' Neelan drank in anger. 'Bollicks to it, I wish it was over!'

There was a harsh scraping sound that might be in the bar or outside of it; a juggernaut out there, maybe, with brakes at metal to metal. But the road was empty. It filled the bar and when it stopped suddenly there was a cold silence and a thud as the Gates of Heaven toppled to the dirt of Brennan's carpet. It sat there like flowers sprouting from a mound of grave-soil.

Calnan crossed to pick it up and rearrange it. He noticed that his wreath hadn't moved. Elmer Devine might be keeping a vigil there with a steadying hand on it. 'Traffic vibration,' he said and Morgan nodded; and conversation flowed back into the stillness. He felt that if he had reached out Devine might clasp his hand and there would be breathless laughter at the mad confusion of ethereal worlds touching like bubbles, ligatured for a moment, and floating apart. Only moments had elapsed and he was back at the counter. Three blanched faces hung like tragic masks before him.

'There's something, isn't there, Cal?' Brennan whispered again. 'I can feel it. Cold as ice.'

'For Christ's sake!' Neelan said; his hands were trembling; he saw that Mackessy was drinking and he retrieved what glasses he could, made a single drink of them, and tossed it back.

'You shouldn't have said it, Neelan!' Brennan hushed his voice in warning.

'Said what?'

'That you wished it was over. Something else too.'

Neelan leant across to him. 'I said bollicks to it!' And as he did, the Gates of Heaven toppled to earth again. Mackessy took off for the toilet.

Neelan said in half a voice as he crept in his wake, 'I'll keep an eye on him.'

'Don't puke in my toilet or you'll be renting a couple of stalls up at the Clincher's,' Calnan said. He felt that Elmer Devine and whatever ghosts were in attendance must stand appalled at the madness they had left behind.

Morgan was restoring the floral tribute, putting damp bar cloths beneath it for grips. Calnan nodded to him, held up a single finger, and as Morgan brought a brandy for Brennan,

167

explosions, two explosions, like gunshots, eructed from the toilet.

'They've committed suicide,' Morgan said.

They came staggering out, shell-shocked, gommy-faced, hands treading air like water. 'Brandy, brandy . . .' Mackessy exposed a wad of money to pull off a ten. 'Doubles!'

'Double doubles,' Neelan said.

'The light bulbs, was it?' Calnan asked.

'How did you know?'

'I was thinking of your father.'

'There was no truth in that,' Neelan confessed longing for forgiveness. 'Just a bit of conversation. Harmless.'

'There's truth in it now.'

'They lit up like fireballs,' Mackessy said. 'White hot! And explosions, dear Christ, we were showered in glass!'

'Get a brush and sweep it up,' Calnan told Brennan.

'I wouldn't go in there with a priest in front of me!' Brennan pleaded.

But Morgan was already on his way with brush and dustpan. 'Trying to see who could piss highest, was it?' he said as he passed.

Calnan found himself somehow comforted by it all: the thought of unseen guests about him, jokes and mischievous laughter, was more reassuring than a million candles and icons.

He sipped his brandy in a warmth of happiness.

Morgan had returned. At the end of the bar he was saying, 'The wiring here is like dust.' He was rubbing thumb and forefinger together. 'Dust.'

Neelan and Mackessy had taken their drinks to the fire; they sat in silence, shock. Calnan bought another brandy for Brennan and drank beer himself. Blondie smiled at him; and Sher: he watched their speed and grace and the lovely movements of their bodies.

In ten minutes it would be opening time and the pace would quicken: he looked at the cleanliness of his shoes, the pressed suit, white cuffs, black tie, and nodded satisfaction to Morgan.

The doorbell rang. Brennan looked fearfully over his shoulder, was locked in immobility.

Calnan opened the door and knew they were the brewery men. Officials, spotters, hatchet men, messenger boys? There were two of them, the Long and the Short. The Short was middle-aged, exuding a kind of smiling hubris; he wore an unremarkable tie and a matching piece peeped from his breast-pocket; he had learned how to polish his shoes too brightly in National Service; he was a clerk by any other name. The Tall was more dangerous, Calnan thought: an unblemished golden face and fashioned long yellow hair adding a raffishness to the sombre costly skill of his tailor.

The Short said, 'Mr Calnan?'

'Yes.'

They were the brewery's men. '. . . your Area Manager, Mr Calnan . . . your Local Director . . . how nice to meet you, Mr Calnan.'

He had waved them in.

The Short, lips pursed, hardly smiling, ignored the bar damage, stared about, seemed to await other explanations.

This was it, Calnan knew, aware of the mission, the smiles, the tactics, the scowls. And, hospitality be damned! He stood and watched them.

He said to the short one eventually. 'Well?'

'What's this, Mr Calnan?'

'A funeral party.'

'But the time!' He looked at his watch. 'In breach of licensing laws, aren't you? Perhaps you have an extension from your local police superintendent?'

The Tall had been surveying the bustle, the staff, the trade, assessing the value of it all. He said with admirable concern. 'It would be nice to chat in private. Upstairs, Mr Calnan?'

Calnan motioned them to lead the way. The Short commented, commentated, as he went. 'These stairs are filthy,

aren't they? . . .' Rubbed his fingers on the scabrous walls.
'. . . crawling . . . the bathroom, Mr Calnan! . . . My God! . . .
what's happened here? . . . these floors . . . your bedroom, Mr
Calnan . . . primitive . . . how do you stand it?'

'I only sleep in it,' Calnan said. 'One place is as good as
another to doss. Publicans live in their bars from year to
year.'

'How many years, Mr Calnan?' the Tall asked.

'Twenty-odd.'

'A long time.' He seemed to be in charge now. 'A lot of
service to the brewery. Makes an unpleasant job even more
difficult. The police called on you last night?'

'Yes,' Calnan said.

'Why?' the short one asked.

Calnan said quietly, 'Don't ask bloody silly questions.'

The tall one was laughing, running fingers through his
yellow hair. Parliamentary cut and thrust! It was good. 'Believe me, Mr Calnan, this is a most unpleasant task for us. To
give summary notice to a man of your standing goes against
the grain.'

'Summary?'

'I'm afraid so. You see, all agreements pertaining to notice
and that kind of thing are void where there is alleged felony.
Alleged, I said. Terrorism, even the smear of it, can't be seen
to be taken lightly by the brewery. Though they may hold
yourself in reasonable esteem. And, however discreetly the
police may move, amazingly, word gets about.'

'Amazingly,' Calnan said.

'Then there is the matter of your criminal record. Not
disclosed. The less said the better. You couldn't have entered
the brewery service with a known criminal record.'

'Or without it,' Calnan said.

'Tomorrow our surveyors and stocktakers will call on you
and do their sums, After that, we'd like you out, instantly, if
possible.' He paused. 'You haven't in mind to defend the situ-
ation, I hope. Believe me, you don't stand an earthly, Mr

Calnan, and it's best not to disturb muddy ponds.' He confided, 'I like the Paddies. I did a couple of tours in Ulster, you see.' He seemed to smile at the memory of it, 'You see?'

'Yes,' Calnan said.

'Tell you what,' he said with a great glow of magnanimity. 'I'll bend the rules a little. Your licence to sell beer, wines and spirits will be valid until midnight, tonight. After that, no more.' He clicked his fingers, smiled. 'The best I can do. Unpleasant orders from your customers, Mr Calnan, you can reject. With my orders, we don't have that privilege. Either of us. And at least you can enjoy your funeral party.'

'Yes.'

'Can we buy you a drink before we go?'

'No,' Calnan said. 'But after midnight if you're passing . . .'

He laughed. 'I'm glad you're taking it in your stride. A distressing job at times. Tears, pleas, people on their knees even. Good day to you, Mr Calnan.'

'Good day,' the little manager-clerk said.

Calnan listened to them descend the stairs and from the window watched their car move into the snake of traffic. Someone, days ago, he felt had stoked and started up an ancient merry-go-round and he sat on a prancing hobby-horse whirling about the shrill steaming poops of the calliope. He looked at the room. It was ugly. The daylight was merciless. And Elmer Devine? How had the Clincher, like God, breathed life into him? Toppling Gates of Heaven, exploding light bulbs. When you were in doubt you looked out into the traffic to banish your ghosts: in hurly-burly there was no room for even a little madness. Ghosts came out at night-time into the still air. Calnan, on his insomniac walks, felt ghosts were everywhere on the quiet sleeping streets. Once, in a back-double, in brilliant moonlight, a couple of hours before dawn, he had seen a man in shirt-sleeves sitting outside his door reading a newspaper. The house was bricked-up and boarded. Calnan had passed in silence, walked into the distance

171

without ever looking back. You couldn't tell people about that: there was no room for even a little madness. He took a long drink of brandy and went down to the bar.

Neelan and Mackessy were at the counter, glowing with drink and confidence restored, momentarily at least.

'Where there's too much distraction a man misses the obvious,' Neelan said. 'Vibration! Of course! Even Morgan saw that and it's near enough sawdust between his ears. A slightly damp cloth is like an adhesive. Stabilises the whole thing.'

'Put your hand on it,' Mackessy advised. 'You'll see what he means.'

'I think I can follow it,' Calnan said; he looked at the counter. 'What about glasses? Did they move?'

'Glasses absorb vibration,' Makessy explained.

'And of course,' Neelan added, 'with the slope of a glass the weight of liquid is concentrated on the bottom.'

'I see,' Calnan said.

'There's a common–sense explanation for everything.' Mackessy could afford to look back in amusement. 'Light bulbs? Bad wiring! If we hadn't so many things on our minds we'd have copped that straightaway.'

Mackessy ordered drinks. 'Have one, Cal,' he said persuasively. 'Duffy's last day!'

'Why not?' Calnan agreed. 'Has anyone contacted his bird at Stoke Newington yet?'

'No address,' Neelan said.

Mackessy wondered about it. 'He was more than cagey about that little piece,' he said.

'There might be a husband in the picture. Or out of it,' Neelan warned.

'I didn't see him as a home-breaker,' Calnan said.

Neelan smiled. 'He'd tip a tart on a trampoline.'

At that moment Brennan was passing the funeral flowers when the table was upturned and the Gates of Heaven sent skittering against the counter. There was laughter above the clamour of conversation. Someone shouted Brennan was pissed again! But Brennan, transfixed for a moment, held up his hands in innocence; then he was in flight to the toilet until he remembered the explosive manifestations for Neelan and Mackessy. He made it to Calnan's private stairs and sat there, limp as a rag.

Neelan said, 'Cack-handed bastard!'

'Too much free drink. Greedy. Can't refuse,' Mackessy explained it.

It was coming up for one forty-five. In fifteen minutes the Clincher's hearse and limousine would be pulling up for the lap of honour before the scarper in the traffic to Finchley.

'I don't think he touched that table,' Calnan said. 'He was feet from it.'

The door swung open. A tall coloured gentleman – hair greying, dignified, scar tissue peeping at the edge of his beard, purple bow tie, a quiet suit – stood before them.

Neelan and Mackessy stood in disarray, seemed to hide behind the bulk of Calnan.

Calnan said pleasantly, 'Are you Elmer Devine?'

The man said in flat West Indian cockney, 'Mini-cab, guv'nor. You have a funeral party?'

'Somewhere there, may be,' Calnan said and pointed. 'Ask around.'

Calnan went out on to the pavements, looked at the daylight on the November street and at the sky, cold, very blue, with torn clouds. It was Duffy's last trip but a good day, he thought.

He felt movement and knew that Neelan and Mackessy had flanked him again.

12

*F*rom the corner Calnan could look west along a quarter
mile of the road to Highbury before, like a country lane,
it meandered out of sight. Traces of old villages, old roads
survived. The wind blew up from Hackney again with the
flap of loose clothing: trouser-legs ballooned and struggled.

'There it is,' Neelan said.

Distantly, a hearse and limousine came into view in the
stream of traffic. Duffy was arriving.

'God rest him,' Mackessy said.

Calnan nodded, glanced at them: they stood shivering in
the wind that he hardly felt. They were pale and frightened,
arrogance in tatters after so many spectral visitations.

'You look like perished pups,' he said.

But they were glad to be in reality of bleak November.
'It's good to get a breath of air,' Mackessy said.

'A fine bracing day,' Neelan agreed.

Calnan looked back over three, four days, and thought that
the whole cycle of existence, the job of being people and
making a mark or a place, had been driven underground
beneath a globe-skin of hammering pistons, a plague of noise:
like a publican in his cellar beneath shuffling feet, he remembered. Were catechisms still chanted in classrooms, he
wondered. Q: who made the world? A: God made the world.
He looked at the neglected pavements beneath his feet, worn
granite kerbstones. You fat slime . . . convicted criminal . . .

Paddies I like, Mr Calnan . . . my mob, a couple of tours . . .
you see . . . you're taking it well . . .

Calnan laughed aloud, startled them.

Neelan jerked. Mackessy said, 'Four weeks to Christmas.'
A red bus crawled by with red Santa and reindeer, somehow,
between decks, bolting at speed through snowflakes and pine
wood.

'Everything in the wrong place,' Calnan said.

The hearse and limousine pulled into the kerbside, the black
figures and drivers and pall-bearers stood as if for inspection.

'Flowers in there,' Calnan said. He could see the coffin-
plate: *Roderick H. O'C. Davis*. No more: unborn, deathless.

He said to Mackessy, 'Get Brennan. He's on the stairs. Don't
shout at him. Tell him it's time.'

The Gates of Heaven were being secured like a triumphal
pediment on the hearse: inside, the wreath was laid on the
coffin-lid; the mourners, in groups, came out to sit in their
cars awaiting the take-off. From the window Morgan raised a
hand to Calnan; across the way Cassie opened her door a
moment and smiled; Wang stood at the takeaway, cleaver in
hand, a menacing wisp.

'Are you feeling all right?' Calnan asked Brennan.

'Yes, Cal.'

'You look poisoned.'

Neelan said, 'Did that mini-cab Spade come out?'

'I don't know,' Calnan told him.

Mackessy shook his head. 'A Spade came in, no Spade came
out.'

Calnan went to inspect. 'Empty bar,' he said. 'Morgan
never saw a Spade or a beard this morning. Come on!'

'Then,' Neelan said, 'Morgan is blind or a liar.'

'I don't think so,' Calnan said; he pointed at the limousine
and the impatient hearse.

The cortège, at a slow respectful pace, made its outdated
circle of the block where village curtains might once have
been drawn and people in shadows would visualise the waxen

face of Duffy that would not be seen on the streets again. But now it was a token journey past blind windows and people, grudged moments before speed was gathered and schedules restored.

Calnan said, 'The mini-cab man'; pointed.

They had left the Trade Winds far behind and suddenly, at an intersection, there was the dignified Negro, head slightly bowed as they passed.

Calnan said, 'Elmer Devine. I think.'

Neelan and Mackessy bent low from public gaze to drink from their bottles; Brennan knelt like a communicant. Silence sat on the endless tedious journey and when the hearse and its crocodile passed the manorial gates at Finchley, moved up the long avenue by parterred blooms and shrubs and manicured grass, Neelan, a little braver, said, 'Credit where credit is due. The place is kept like a bowling green.'

Mackessy nodded. 'A fair job.'

Brennan sat, fist to lips.

Calnan, without care or formality, drank from his bottle. Wild overgrown graveyards with rusted iron gates and wind always brushing or blowing across them had more welcome and comfort. The great stone building came in view – it might be casino or swimming pool – and, on the acres of gravelled parking space about it, cortèges and capsules of grief awaited their allotted moments of churchtime and prayerspeak. In, out: a sausage machine at work, and further away pale smoke bled from a chimney.

'Some of the drivers make four trips a day here,' Neelan said.

'Canteens, of course,' Mackessy pointed out. 'Toilets, washrooms, the lot. They can make a drop, fit in a pie and chips, and get back for the next load.'

Calnan gave Brennan the brandy bottle and shielded him while he drank. He felt a kind of gentle sorrow for him. And then they were summoned, like a small army crunching their way to a mortuary chapel.

176

'I never saw so many hearses,' Neelan said. 'I counted eight.'

Mackessy said, 'And how many on the road? Coming in on the spokes of a wheel.'

Closeness to death and departure had somehow stabilised them: dead bodies ousted incorporeal ghosts. Only Brennan was silent.

But Brennan, revived by brandy, suddenly said, 'There must be mistakes made in a place like this.'

Mackessy said, 'I was at a do once and there's six coffins laid out like a supermarket. We didn't know who we were praying for until he shook the holy water.'

'What about ashes?' Neelan flung down. 'They must have stockpiles like sand and gravel back there.' He nodded towards the smoke. 'You could have Jack the Lad's dust under your mother's picture and saying the odd prayer as you passed . . . Christ!'

Calnan silenced them, Brennan bowed his head, as they entered a place of pews and a pulpit, with all the warmth of a redundant whistle-stop. Duffy's remains sat on a conveyor belt that was poorly disguised as a catafalque and organ music, faint, atonal, crept out from some hidden speaker.

A soutaned and surpliced figure mounted the pulpit and smiled on them. He was a tall distinguished Negro.

Calnan saw the greying temples, the dignity, the little scar sitting beside the darkness of his beard. 'My friends,' he said in such soft unhurried tones that even extraneous sounds were banished and silence was complete. '. . . We have come, not to read the words of strangers . . . or to recite them . . . or in fear of what we call death . . . we have come on a joyous occasion . . . to laugh, smile, call out greetings . . . these are the mortal remains of Roddy Davis soon to pass out of sight . . . but Roddy is standing down there . . . standing among you . . . walking towards me now . . . standing again . . . to face you . . . he asks me to thank you for coming . . . raise your hands and smile to him . . . call out to him!' The chapel was full of sound and moving arms. Calnan looked at the huge span of his hand as he held it aloft. Brennan was in tears of relief, gratitude. When silence had returned the kind American voice said, 'Thank you for coming.' He waved and the coffin drifted out beyond the curtains and silent doors. 'Thank you,' he said. 'I am Elmer Devine.' He came down from the pulpit and entered a vestry door. The congregation, a little rapt, Calnan thought, moved out in pleasant disorder, somehow unsurprised, undisturbed. Neelan and Mackessy smiled wanly: it could have been a shadow of penitence before bright light shone on them.

Brennan said, 'I could feel Jim Duffy was there.'

They nodded.

Neelan said to Calnan: 'Should we go in? The vestry. Pay our respects to Elmer Devine?'

'I don't think you'd find anyone,' Calnan said.

They moved out into the light and the gravelled acres. The limousine awaited them. The November wind swept up over the cropped grass and winter flowers. The plumed yew trees were black as pitch. Beneath one, two silhouetted figures stood still as a momument and, as the limo sped on, Calnan had a momentary glimpse. The Carters, he knew. Lucinda and Idris. He didn't forget faces.

When eventually they were moving on the fast lane of the carriageway towards the East End and the Trade Winds, Calnan said:

'I don't want to talk about it. Forget it. It was a good send-off.' They sat in silence, relief like a pleasant tiredness leaning on them.

Morgan was in command at the Trade Winds; Blondie and Sher, fresh as angels. It was after four. In breach of licensing laws, Calnan thought. The mourners had arrived, were arriving: it would be a lively evening.

'The Trade Winds is like home.' Neelan even smiled.

'Not for long,' Calnan said. He gave Morgan five twenties for the kitty.

'Drinks on the house until further notice,' Morgan announced and said quietly to Neelan, 'Or should I say, "Gentlemen, Mr Neelan and Mr Mackessy are your hosts"?'

'On the house will do fine,' Neelan said.

Mackessy agreed.

Brennan crossed himself.

'Safer, I think,' Morgan said. He took a long look at Neelan before he went for drinks.

Public house evenings start with a strange reluctance to drink, even faintly expressed dislike of drink with offended lips and eyes. And then talk comes and grows and needs punctuation. The end is *Finnegans Wake*.

Ari came with the food at half-past four.

'A drink?' Calnan said.

'Soon,' Ari nodded: a little lip of stomach crept over his belt; he sweated. From his van he carried in trestle tables and white paper cloths. The food was Ari's canvas of design and colour: reds, browns, yellows, a half-dozen greens. The fresh aromas drifted across the counter of oven-baked bread, meats, cucumber, peppers, chutney, onion, pickle, mustard; eggs and tomatoes stuffed to the brim with herbs and pâté; and pastry, gold like Ari's skin.

He arranged it, presented it, bowed to the applause, brought to Calnan a special plate. They drank brandy and Calnan looked at the thick slices of cold lamb with just the faintest edge of fat, potatoes showered in mint, onion rings everywhere and here and there little ponds of chutney and pickle; fresh beetroots, soft warm bread rolls.

'All right, Cal?'

Calnan smiled.

Ari, with the enthusiasm of a swaying *aficionado*, watched him eat, laughing, vicariously tasting and swallowing the mouthfuls. They raised glasses.

'Good?'

'Good.'

With great happiness Ari looked about. 'You, me, Cal,' he

179

said, 'we make money anywhere. The cases down there?' He pointed to the cellar. 'The cases, Cal, the spirits? You want I should move 'em out?'

'Tomorrow,' Calnan said.

Ari pointed at the clock, made a countdown for Calnan. 'Smoke and coffee now at Ari's and soon, like that!' he made a huge finger-snap, 'dinner time and back room for the Big Boys! You see?' He stood in mock sorrow. 'Hard life. No sleep for us, Cal. But, money!'

'What do I owe?' Calnan said. 'The food?'

'Paid for,' Ari said. 'The big black man! Twenty-dollar bills. Pay more than you, Cal!'

Ari, laughing, was gone: short, rapid steps, fat buttocks shaking; even the van seemed to move away with the drive of Ari's enthusiasm.

Calnan looked at the bar again, listened to its noise like a raging bloodstream. A long time ago, he thought, when there were brewing-men in the breweries, it wasn't the trick they had made of it now: milking machines plugged to so many udders and even the milk skimmed. Calnan didn't like yellow-haired adventurers or unemotional little coppers and their minders. He made his rounds, circled the bar, to talk, to nod, to have a drink, move on. In the early evening pause for breath, Morgan had rested; and rested his staff; and now, in the late evening, with hardly an hour to closing, they seemed to be effortlessly in charge. Brennan was a quiet man, pale from the day's convulsion, unremitting in his journeys with swab and glasses. Calnan wondered if it might be a change for the best. And Neelan and Mackessy: they were modest heroes, shrugging at the littleness of their effort and generosity but pie-eyed and fairly screwed now by dint of free-loading. Calnan couldn't remember when he had seen them buy a drink.

Now, glasses in hand, they came to entertain him again.

'Who did the food?' Mackessy asked.

'Elmer Devine.'

Neelan said, 'Ah, for Christ's sake!'

'Paid Ari in twenty-dollar bills.'

'There's a joker wild,' Neelan said again in lickerish bravado. 'And I'll find him!' Even through boozy eyes his disdain of Calnan showed. 'I'll find the bastard!'

'You might stir up a few ghosts.'

Neelan was drunk enough to say, 'Bollicks to the ghosts!' And Mackessy laughed.

'And another thing,' Neelan said. 'That kitty didn't last much more than an hour. You put a ton in, I suppose?'

'I did.'

'An hour and ten minutes,' Mackessy said. 'I timed it.'

'Did you?'

Neelan sensed anger. 'No reflection on present company, of course! But that Welsh billy-goat is tricky. You have him taped, I'm sure.'

'You should tell him,' Calnan said.

'He has it off with his little scrubbers in there at the flick of a zip. They cost him ten flags a jump, did you know that?'

'Ten?'

'He only thinks with his nuts,' Mackessy said. 'Half the manor is screwed. Built like a stallion, down in the southern region. He's slashing in the john one day and you never saw such steam and suds! A bad animal for a pub.'

'I must think about that,' Calnan said.

He waved them away and turned back to his drink: if he set Morgan on them the punishment would be condign and bloody . . .

The towels were long up and Morgan bolting his doors when Neelan said, 'You can give us thirty minutes of your valuable time, I hope, Cal?'

Calnan thought about it, looked at the empty littered bar, the pall of smoke. After a long day, Blondie and Sher were off, waving to him from the door. Morgan poured himself a rum and stood at the counter.

181

'We might have to adjust that job upstairs a bit,' Neelan said. 'Moneywise, you know?'

'I see.'

'Dramatically, you could say.'

'That's good,' Calnan said. 'I thought you over-priced it a bit.'

And in that moment of silence Cassie tapped on the window and Calnan went to meet her. On the pavement she said, 'I'm late. A few words in your ear?'

Calnan brought her towards the furthest end of the bar, out of sight, out of earshot, and, as she passed, Morgan handed her a tapering glass of orange juice. Neelan, chin to chest, hunched in his chair.

Calnan sat her by the window where the traffic noise was ceaseless, alternating spells of more or less decibels, but never silence.

'Do a scan job for me, Cal?'

He nodded.

'This one's for a minder,' she said. 'Big, tough, hard, a few years in the game, misses nothing, makes it pay . . .'

'Do you like him?' Calnan said.

'Yeah.'

'Then forget it.'

Cassie laughed. 'I want you, Calnan! I want a headman in my place! . . . my holy ground!'

Calnan looked at the clock creeping up to midnight. 'Five minutes and I have no licence,' he told her.

'I have a licence.'

Calnan smiled, shook his head. 'I thought I'd take a rest after all the years,' he said. 'A lot of years.'

'Rest'd kill you!'

'I know.'

'You'd be on an earner, Cal. Nice oak-panelled flat where you can hear the old vicar shaking his chains and the clientele special.'

'Business men.'

'Of course.' She put a bunch of keys on the table and pushed it across. 'Tell you what! You go down on your jack, Cal, walk the ground and look around! Then tell me. Promise?'

Calnan raised his hand, and, while the next herd of traffic thundered past, he saw in the glass porch of his entrance the same painted motionless silhouette, a monument, that he had seen by the yew tree at Finchley.

He brought Cassie to the fire.

'Good evening,' she said to all. 'Good evening, Mr Neelan. You've been a naughty boy, fighting, I can see.'

Relief brought almost honesty to Neelan's face.

'Open the door,' Calnan said to Brennan. 'We have visitors.'

It was a grand entrance. He had forgotten how beautiful Lucinda Carter was and how austere her spouse. They bowed with what now seemed an outlandish courtesy.

'Mr Calnan,' Lucinda said, 'we came to apologise. You called on us and you had only gone when there was such turbulence that we knew we had erred. We knew it. Forgive us.'

Calnan presented them. 'Friends of the deceased,' he said and remembered: 'You like a glass of port, I think.'

Morgan brought a tray and precious brittle glasses from his cabinet.

Lucinda said, 'Roddy – Roderick Hodder O'Callaghan Davis – who left us today, was a gifted medium, you see . . .'

In the vacuum Mackessy lauded him. 'He could turn his hand to most things.'

'I'm sure of it,' Lucinda agreed. 'But, as a medium, among the most sensitive. Faultless voice patterns, you see. And even languages. Friends from abroad besieged us for sittings . . .'

'Languages,' Neelan said: the everyday normalcy of Lucinda's chatter gave him sudden courage to destroy. 'Even good friends wouldn't call him a scholar.'

'Mediums, Mr Neelan,' Lucinda said, remembering his name without effort, 'are often the most humble people with

183

no conception of their gifts. And, after a sitting, oblivious of the immediate past.' She smiled. 'But, at moments, they are a sensitive fabric between our worlds.'

Calnan became aware of the stillness: the traffic passed outside in silence, the fire had no breath: Neelan, Mackessy, Brennan, were grouped where the heat-glow caught their tired tranquil faces, the bar pilot light fell on Morgan's hands cupped about his glass: Cassie, in the window beam, was half in silhouette, breaking the flow of street light. The Carters held the stage.

Lucinda said, 'We are eight and almost nine.' Her fingers seemed to touch on a gossamer wall and her eyes searched beyond it. 'Roddy is almost here. He stands out there in shadow, perhaps happy, perhaps a little sad.' The Carters clasped hands, stood, heads bowed, almost dissolving in the twilight: it was a timeless unrecorded space until she spoke again; it was a whisper; her fingers barely stirred the air. 'Something that was Roddy's will draw him close to us.' Her glance moved with infinite slowness from face to face, assessing, discarding. Neelan and Mackessy sat calm and devout as ageing saints, watching her come towards them. 'Bring him close, bring him close,' she whispered: her hands traced some aura that framed them, brushed along the fabric of their sleeves. They seemed to await the signal of her smile to pile on the table what notes and coin they had. 'Roddy is here.' She watched him circle the bar and return. 'He's here beside you . . . but going now . . . going . . . soon at rest.'

The traffic noises crept back, the hoarse flame of the fire. The Carters left and Calnan saw no shadows on the window; the port was untouched.

'We'll call it a day,' he said; he stood at the door, ample host, trencherman, touching their shoulders as they left.

Duffy was gone too; he had lingered a while and was gone.

Calnan shut the door, looked at the piled money on the table. A lot of money. He gathered it and climbed the stairs to what was no longer his red room. Ugly, he thought again.

He took the bar takings from under his pillow and there was a fresh half-bottle of brandy. He drank, smoothed and folded his notes; made a neat fold of Duffy's whip and put it with what he had already recovered. There was a precise arrangement of everything in his safe.

Calnan did his sums and reckoned it had cost him two ton plus to keep Duffy out of a common grave. The showpiece bathroom, of course, would have made it about even-stephen but you couldn't win them all.

He took the neat parcel of plague bones, locked his safe, and went out into the small hours. The time! The Carters seemed to have spent only minutes but it was in the last quarter before three o'clock. He drank again and stepped out into the darkness and the sudden flurries of wind.

At Mare Street, Hackney, he posted the plague bones.

There used to be horse fairs in Mare Street, he thought; and a stream and a bridge by the churchyard; and coach-builders worked in Hackney; there had been a well in Well Street. He walked down the long road by Victoria Park, crossed the Old Ford and Roman Roads and the Mile End and on to Limehouse and East Stepney.

Cassie's rectory in its trees and climbing weeds, surrounding walls, chained gates, appeared suddenly as he rounded the curve of some old unplanned street.

He walked the grounds first, pushing through the tall dry decay of November: leafless elms and birches were roots gripping into the winter sky; he could hear the scrape of wind. There was a roofed lych-gate and a stile.

Inside, when he walked the corridors again, he was conscious of great embrasured windows and tailored shutters that would be barred at night. Somewhere the twigs of a branch tapped on glass. And a stairway led to a tiny turret room where he sat for a long time and looked out at his parish. People might have prayed there, he thought, before dawns crept in or in the late evenings a long time ago.

He drank and felt warmth. He locked doors and gateway

and walked down to Narrow Street and Limehouse. Nothing could destroy the beauty of the River: a string of barges moved down with the tide and lights were strung out here and there across in Rotherhithe and Bermondsey and down by the long foreshore of the Isle of Dogs.

Behind, and flanking him, were the old streets and wharves where the famine ships had come to boozers and brothels; and just out there was the mud where whippers had groped for coal and scrap. The friendly ghosts were still around. The tide had turned, the wind was fighting against it. He dropped the possessions of James Duffy-Davis and his entire wealth, one pound thirty-eight and a half pence, into the darkness of the water.

At nine he would take a taxi to Ari's, ring Cassie's number . . . He began methodically to plan his day.